THE LAND KILLER

THE LAND KILLER

LEE HOFFMAN

SAGEBRUSH
Large Print Westerns

First published in Great Britain by Hale
First published in the United States by Doubleday

Published in Large Print 2007 by ISIS Publishing Ltd.,
7 Centremead, Osney Mead, Oxford OX2 0ES
United Kingdom
by arrangement with
Golden West Literary Agency

British Library Cataloguing in Publication Data
Hoffman, Lee, 1932–
    The land killer. – Large print ed. –
(Sagebrush western series)
1. Western stories
2. Large type books
I. Title
813.5'4 [F]

ISBN 978–0–7531–7766–2 (hb)

Printed and bound in Great Britain by
T. J. International Ltd., Padstow, Cornwall

To: Terry Hughes

CHAPTER
ONE

There had been rain during the night. The air was crisp and clear. The long meadow grasses sparkled with drops of water caught in their tender blades. The sun, still low over the eastern peaks, cast hazy blue shadows. Aspen forests fringing the meadow twinkled in the morning breeze. The grass rippled lightly. This was fine land, vital with life. Land full of promise.

Across the Casey River, the land was dying. Murdered.

As he rode, Dutch Falke thought he would die himself before he would let the Falcon range be murdered in the same way.

He knew Quint Leslie wanted his land. Quint wanted to take it and use it and strip it the way he was doing to his own range. Dutch wondered how long it would be before Quint made a move to get it.

The horse under Dutch's saddle was a sorrel filly, a new horse to Falcon. Where the trail cut straight and level across the meadow, he set it into a rack. Its head bobbed and its hoofs fell into the quick rhythm of the gait. A rack was smooth and enjoyable for a rider, but tiring for a horse. Dutch was pleased by the steady strength he felt in the lithe body of the filly.

According to the papers he got when he bought it, the filly had been sired by a pacing stud on a Morgan mare in the bluegrass country back East. It was a responsive animal, with a light mouth and easy gaits. He thought it would make a good gift for his bride-to-be. Herr Onkel Heinrich said the girl could ride well.

What was she like, this girl from Hesse, Dutch wondered. He had never met her. She had been a mere child when he left Germany for America sixteen years ago. Herr Onkel wrote that she was strong and pretty, well trained in the arts of housekeeping, and well educated for a female. He had assured Dutch she would make a good wife for him.

Dutch hoped Herr Onkel was right. He didn't like the arrangement. He would have preferred to pick his own wife. But he was deeply indebted to Herr Onkel Heinrich. He would accept Herr Onkel's choice.

A sound startled him from his thoughts. Someone had shouted nearby. Someone else gave a shout in answer. Hoofs thudded against the earth.

The noise was coming from beyond the upthrust of rock that cut across the meadow ahead of Dutch. Men were driving horses there. But Dutch hadn't ordered any horses driven on this part of the range. His crew was miles away, gathering and branding the spring calves. No one had any business working horses on this part of his land.

He thought they must be Quill riders, Quint Leslie's men. Drawing his revolver, he checked the loads. Then he threw the filly into a gallop.

The upthrust of rock that angled across the meadow had a gentle slope on the side toward Dutch. It dropped in a sharp bank at the other side. The trail crossed at its low end. He swung the filly toward the crossing. As he topped the slope, he saw the men and the horses.

A young mustang stud with some score of mares and spring colts had been run up against the ridge where it was high and steep. The horses couldn't climb it. They milled at its base as two men on horseback worked to hold them trapped.

It was a hard job for the mounts. They were heavy feather-legged bays that looked more like a wagon team than saddle stock. The saddles on them were old army issue. The men in the saddles were young, gangly, long-boned men dressed in faded canvas and cotton, with wool hats flopping on their heads. A third young man, similarly dressed, was afoot. He had a lasso rope in his hand. Building a loop, he tossed it at the wild stud.

The throw was unskilled and awkward. The loop closed before it reached the end of the rope. It made no difference. The stud spun away as the loop left the roper's hand. The man had failed to anticipate any move by the horse.

At the sight of them, Dutch knew they couldn't be Quill riders. Quint Leslie would never hire such men, or send them out on such mounts. They looked like farmers. Clod-hoppers, the cowhands called this kind. What were clod-hoppers doing here, chasing *his* wild horses?

3

"Hold!" he shouted, gigging the filly over the crest of the slope. His voice was strong, and heavily accented. Despite all his years of trying, he had never completely mastered the language of America. "Hold there! What the hell you do?"

The young men gave him quick, casual glances. None of them answered him. The two riders shoved their lumbering mounts on toward the mustangs, trying to separate the stud from the mares. A pinto mare with a long-legged colt at her heels ducked past them.

The man afoot rebuilt his loop. He tried again for the stud. The rope snapped out more like a cracking bullwhip than a catch rope. The loop flew from his hand. The bitter end seemed to be tied around his waist.

Dutch scowled with amazement at such foolishness. The fact that the men were bothering his mustangs angered him. Their apparent incompetence disgusted him. Lifting his gun, he triggered a shot into the air.

That got their attention.

The two on horseback reined in, facing Dutch. The one on foot left his loop lie as it had fallen. More of the milling mustangs broke to run after the escaping mare. The stud paused, pawing the ground. It was a piebald, more black than white, with broad shoulders and a well-rounded rump. A good stud. Neck arched, hide gleaming with sweat, it snorted its defiance.

"What the hell you think you are do?" Dutch demanded as he rode toward the men.

"What the hell is it to you?" one shouted back at him.

4

The mustang stud was dancing nervously, its attention on the horsemen. It was backing away from them. Toward the rope that lay, loop open, on the ground. One of the riders noticed. He edged his mount toward the stud.

The stud took another step back. A hind hoof touched earth within the loop.

"Stony! Now!" the rider hollered.

The man afoot saw and understood. With a jerk, he closed the loop around the stud's fetlock.

Dutch tried to call out a warning. The men paid him no heed.

At the feel of the tightening rope, the stud jumped. It was astraddle the rope. Head ducked, it kicked. The rope snapped taut. The stud fell. So did the roper.

The stud was the first to scramble up. It had managed to kick its hoof out of the loop, but it had gotten the rope tangled around its neck and across its chest. Legs free, it ran.

The man with the bitter end of the rope around his waist was suddenly being dragged wildly over the ground.

One of the horsemen snatched a pistol from his belt.

Dutch was already moving. The saddle he rode was his regular rig, a double-barreled Texas roping kack, and the rope was ready, tied hard, as always. He let his revolver fall from his hand as he grabbed the throw rope. The filly was no cow pony, but it was quick. It answered his rein. He thought it had brain and gut

5

enough for the job. He rolled his loop down the rope, aiming it to be open in front of the stud's plunging head.

The farmer fired.

The stud's muzzle was into Dutch's loop. The rope was closing as the stud fell. The horse hit the ground with Dutch's loop snugging around its neck.

The farmer fired again.

And again.

"Stop, dammit!" Dutch shouted.

The stud gave one toss of its head, trying to shake away the rope and the sudden pain. Its eyes showed white-rimmed, still defiant. It tried to snort. The sound came as a weak gurgle. Red foam bubbled from its nostrils. Its head fell to the ground, the eyes blank and empty.

The man who had been fool enough to tie his rope around his own waist, and had gone for a hard ride because of it, lay on his belly groaning.

One rider dropped from his horse to hurry to the downed man. The farmer with the pistol stayed in his saddle. He called out, "Stony, you hurt?"

"Sure I'm hurt!" the one on the ground answered. Sitting up, he bellowed, "Hell! Hell and brimstone! That horse done like to pulled me apart!"

Dutch glanced from the man, Stony, to the ground the stud had dragged him across. It was thickly grassed and thoroughly rain-damp. Stony had left his mark in crushed grass blades and smeared mud, but apparently he hadn't suffered any serious injury.

The farmer who had dismounted squatted at his side. He looked Stony over thoughtfully, worked his jaw, spat, and said, "That big old nose of yours done plowed a fine furrow."

Stony answered with a grunt.

The filly under Dutch shuffled restlessly, troubled by the noise of the shots and the scents of gunpowder and fresh blood. He could feel the fear in it. He felt trust as well. Despite its fear, the filly stood to his command. He gave it a pat on the withers and slid out of the saddle.

Hunkering beside the dead mustang, he touched its head respectfully. That had been a proud head. A wild free head. Now it was only hide and bone and meat growing cold, all because three clodhoppers were fools.

He looked up at the man with the pistol. "Damn you, is no need to kill!"

Moving his horse toward Dutch, the man replied, "Mister, that studhorse was near about to kill my brother!"

"I had on it the rope. I could be stop it."

"What the hell you care? It ain't your horse!"

"Yeah!" Stony agreed. Getting to his feet, he staggered toward Dutch. "Yeah, that there damn horse meant to kill me!"

"The horse is only want to be free. That is all," Dutch said.

"I'd 've had him if he hadn't 've fell down and got the rope from me," Stony grumbled, as if the horse's freedom had been a personal challenge to him.

"Is not be your horse to take," Dutch answered.

The third farmer spoke up. "Them there is *wild* horses, mister! They belong to anybody as can catch them!"

Dutch shook his head in denial. He glanced from the corner of an eye at the mares. They had all run. They were disappearing into the distance. At least they were safe now.

He said, "The wild horses belong to the land. This is Falcon land. No one has right to be take them off this land."

"They don't belong to nobody," the third farmer protested. "That's what we was told. These here horses without any brands on them don't belong to nobody!"

Dutch gestured at the eastern-bred filly. "This horse is not have brand on it, but it is mine."

"Not if it ain't got no brand," Stony replied. "We heard it all in town. Out here a horse without no brand is free to whoever takes him. We need horses, so we been hunting us some. I ain't got none at all. Wade and Rob here ain't got much of ones." He pointed at the others as he named them. The one with the pistol was Wade. The other was Rob. Stony appeared to be the youngest, and Wade the oldest. All looked like brothers.

Wade backed up Stony. "That's right! A man in town done explained it all to us. Any horse what ain't got a brand on it and is running loose out here in these hills belongs to anybody as can take it!"

"No!" Dutch snapped. He knew that, by law, the wild mustangs on the open range might belong to any man who could capture them. He knew that he held no legal title to the horses, or to a good part of the land

8

they ran on. But by custom, by the right of years of possession, he claimed the land and every animal on it. They were his to use, and his responsibility to protect.

Anger thickened his accent as he shouted, "Horses you want, somewhere else you go! From off Falcon range you stay! You hear me?"

Stony nudged Rob. "Hey, he talks kinda funny, don't he?"

Rob nodded in agreement. Suddenly he looked worried. Leaning toward Stony, he whispered, "You don't reckon maybe he's that wild Dutchman we was warned about? The one that hangs folks?"

Stony's face stiffened as he stared at Dutch. Slowly and cautiously, as if he feared Dutch might do something to him while he wasn't looking, he shifted his gaze from Dutch to Wade.

Wade was still on horseback, still holding the gun. He hadn't heard Rob's whisper.

Dutch had heard it. He was hunkered beside the dead stud. With taut deliberateness, he rose. In his high-heeled Texas boots, with his spine rigid and his head up, he towered over the two brothers who were afoot.

He spoke carefully, trying to subdue his accent. Anger was icy in his voice. "I am Bartel Falke. This is my range. All on it is mine to protect. The wild horses are mine. This horse you have murdered is my horse. You will go from off my land. You will not be come back from off the road while you are by this side of the river. Do you understand me?"

The three farmers exchanged fearful glances, questioning each other.

"Ain't no crazy Dutchman gonna hang me!" Rob shouted suddenly. He lunged at Dutch, both arms out in front of him. His hands rammed into Dutch's chest. "Get him, Wade!"

The unexpected thrust staggered Dutch. Dancing for footing on the slick grass, he swung a fist at Rob's gut. Off balance, he couldn't get much force into the blow. Rob barely winced as the knuckles hit.

"I can't get him!" Wade screeched, waving his pistol. "You're in the way!"

Catching his footing, Dutch side-stepped to keep Rob between himself and the gun. Stony jumped behind him and grabbed for his arms. Dutch wheeled, swinging. This time, Dutch was balanced and there was power driving his fist. It struck into Stony's ribs, rocking the farmer back on his heels.

But now Rob was behind Dutch.

Rob flung his arms around Dutch, trying for a bear hug that would lock Dutch's arms against his sides. Dutch rammed back with his elbows. He grazed Rob hard enough to bring a sharp grunt. And to ease the sudden grip. Twisting as he pulled away, he swung at Rob. His fist slammed into the soft part of Rob's belly. Rob doubled over, clutching himself as he backed away. Dutch moved quickly to close on him.

Something rammed Dutch in the back of one leg. A hobnail boot. Stony was behind him, kicking at him. As Dutch swiveled to defend himself, the boot hit him again. It drove into his knee. The knee folded. Dutch felt himself falling. He grabbed at Stony as he went down, trying to drag the farmer with him.

Stony kicked again. This time he rammed upward with his knee, slamming it into Dutch's chest.

Dutch lost his grip on Stony. Hitting ground, he rolled onto his belly and braced to scramble to his feet. A weight piled onto his back, crushing his face down to the earth. One of the farmers had leaped astride him.

Hands pressed to the ground, Dutch bucked his body against the weight. He hoped he could throw the man off. Twisting, wrenching, he tried to pull free.

The man on his back shouted, "Put him down! Stony! Wade! Help me! I can't hardly hold him!"

Suddenly pain smashed through Dutch's head. Stony had kicked him in the temple.

Stony kicked again.

Dutch felt the blows hammering into his skull. Each was a red explosion driving him toward darkness. He made another effort to unseat the farmer and realized it was futile. The blows kept coming, ramming the strength out of him. The darkness was overwhelming him.

He understood that if the farmers meant to kill him, he couldn't stop them now. He let himself go limp.

The vicious boot blows to his head ceased. The pain didn't. It kept pounding at him with each beat of his heart. The darkness kept pushing in on him.

As if from far away, he heard a voice. "Oh, God! We've killed him!"

But they hadn't, he thought dimly. As the darkness took him, he was certain he would wake again.

CHAPTER
TWO

The sun was warm on Dutch's back. With awareness of the warmth came awareness of pain. His head felt stuffed with crushed rock. Heavy sharp-cutting shards of stone that ground into his being with each beat of his heart.

He lay still awhile, listening to small sounds and sampling the scents in the air. There was fresh grass under his face. Dried blood close by. A buzzing of flies. A sound of something small scurrying through the grass. But no suggestion of men, or of horses.

He forced open his eyes. It took effort to lift himself onto his hands and knees. Squinting, he looked around.

Flies swarmed over the carcass of the mustang stud. A pair of buzzards perched on a rock nearby, eying him, wanting him to move away from the cold meat.

His saddle lay on the ground, with his bridle next to it. The sorrel filly was gone. So were the three farmers. The saddle had the Falcon brand burned into the skirt. The filly had never worn a brand.

With a faint grunted curse in German, Dutch got himself on to his feet. He took a few tentative steps. His head spun as he bent to pick up the saddle. Ribs aching with every breath he dragged into his lungs, he began to walk.

Astride the fast-racking filly, the trip from the ranch house to the place where he encountered the farmers had been a short one. Afoot, with his saddle heavy on his shoulder and his head thick with pain, Dutch found it a hell of a long walk home. By the time he caught sight of the house, every muscle, every bone of his body protested each move he made.

The house sat on a broad step of land against the rise of a high ridge. Behind it, a cliff cut sharply upward, giving it protection from the icy north winds in winter. In front of it, the ground rolled in a gentle slope of cleared land, a good meadow and a wide yard for outbuildings and corrals.

The house was built of stone, squat and massive, with the appearance of a fortress. When Dutch built it, he had felt the need of a fortress in this wild land.

Wearily, he walked upslope, across the yard, past the empty corrals and outbuildings, on to the empty house. The silence seemed strange and lonely. Every ranch hand and almost all of the horses were at spring roundup. Until the day before, Dutch had been with them, amid the ruckus of gathering and branding the calves. If Herr Onkel Heinrich had waited just one more week before sending the girl, Dutch could have stayed on and seen the job done. But there had been some confusion, and Hannchen Gerber was on her way a week too soon.

Dutch resented the interruption.

He wasn't worried about the roundup. He knew the foreman, Slim Walker, could handle it. Slim had been with him ever since Dutch drove his first herd into these mountains. Slim knew the work as well as he did. But Dutch felt that the work was his to share. And he liked it.

He enjoyed the feel of a good horse between his legs and a rope in his hand. He liked the taste of strong, hot coffee under the stars after a hard day of riding. He looked forward to making the final tally that would tell him what to hope for in the fall when the beef was sold.

But the girl was important. Sixteen years ago, Herr Onkel Heinrich had promised him a bride.

Sixteen years ago, young Bartel Falke had left his homeland for a new life. From the day he had been orphaned and Herr Onkel Heinrich had taken him in, there had been talk of America. Herr Onkel had worked and scrimped and saved to send young Bartel to the new land.

When the day had come at last, and young Bartel stood on the dock waiting to board the ship for America, he had been very nervous and excited. He had hardly listened as Herr Onkel Heinrich repeated much of the advice he had given during the months of preparation for the trip.

And then Herr Onkel had added, "When you are rich and successful in America, I will send you a wife. A good husky young Hessian girl to keep your house and bear your sons."

At the time, Bartel had accepted the promise with little thought. His mind had been occupied with the frightening prospect of seeking his fortune alone in a strange land.

During the past sixteen years, he had learned that the land wasn't frightening. It was awesome and demanding, but it paid him well for his labor. The first six years of hard work and good luck had given him a stake and a trade.

He had learned the cattle business from the back of a mustang. He had acquired cattle of his own. Ten more years had turned a slender foothold on the frontier into a secure stronghold. Now his brand, the Falcon, was second only to Quint Leslie's in these mountains. And even if everyone did call him "Dutch" instead of his real name, and did whisper unpleasant things about him behind his back, they took off their hats and spoke with respect to Bartel Falke's face.

Now, crossing the narrow gallery to the house, he thought it would be a good thing to have a wife. A very fine thing to have a woman of his own to warm his bed and mend his clothes and prepare good Hessian foods that he hadn't tasted since he left his homeland.

He dropped the saddle on the gallery and shoved open the door. There was a bootjack just inside. He tugged off his boots. Leaving them lie, he padded to a chair by the fireplace and slumped into it.

The living room of the ranch house was big, spanning the width of the building. The fireplace at one end was large enough for a whole calf to be spitted and roasted in it. The chairs that were ranked facing the fireplace were simple and sturdy and comfortable. Brass spittoons were handy to the chairs.

The far wall of the room was lined with shelves, well stocked with books. Long winters gave a man a lot of time for reading. It didn't take many winters snowed in at line camps to make him weary of reading the labels on airtights.

In the middle of the room was a large trestle table flanked by hide-bottomed chairs.

The kitchen and three bedrooms opened into the living room. Two of the bedrooms had been occupied by the foreman and the cook. But now their gear was at the bunkhouse. The emptied bedrooms would serve for Hannchen and her chaperone until the wedding. In time, Dutch hoped they would become bedrooms for children.

Sinking deep into the chair, stretching his weary legs out in front of him, he wished that Hannchen were already there. It would be good to have someone go light a fire under the coffeepot for him. Good to have someone comfort his aches. Good to have the trip into town to meet Hannchen over and done with.

But for now, there was no one to serve him but himself, and the day was aging fast. He had much to do yet. The coach would not wait for his muscles to rest and his bruises to heal. He had to meet it at sundown. Today, of all days.

After a short, inadequate rest, he hauled himself from the chair and fixed a meal of sorts. By the time he had finished eating, the water in the stove reservoir was warm. He bathed, then dressed in his good suit.

Standing in front of the mirror, he considered his image critically. He wanted to appear at his best when Hannchen saw him for the first time.

The suit looked fine. But not his face. That clodhopper's boot had cut a gash in his forehead from the brow up into the hairline. A lot of skin had been peeled away. A puffy patch of discolored flesh was swelling around the gash.

It was a poor face to greet a new bride with, he thought. But there wasn't anything he could do about it.

Setting his hat squarely on his head, he went out to saddle himself a horse.

Ten years ago, when Dutch Falke had first crossed the Casey River with a small crew of freedmen and half-breeds, pushing a scraggly herd of Texas scrubs ahead of them, Newt's Ford had been a trading post for Indians and trappers, and a way station for wagons headed west. The Indians had camped across the road from the way station on the ground where the First Cattlemen's Bank now stood. Quint Leslie was the one who had driven the Indians away and turned Newt's Ford from a way station into a town.

Quint Leslie was a hard-shelled Texan who had arrived in the area with a crew and a large herd of longhorns a couple of years after Dutch settled on the west side of the Casey River. Quint spread his herd out along the east side, built his headquarters on a good slope, and dug in his heels.

He hadn't been content with just running cattle. He had induced the stagecoach line to use the Newt's Ford road by building a bridge across the Casey River. When the old trading post was torn down, to be replaced by a hotel and coach station, Quint built a sawmill to supply the material. He brought in crews to cut the timber and mill it. When the station was finished, he bought wagons and hired teamsters and shipped lumber to other settlements. When he found coal on his side of the river, he brought in more workmen and started stripping it.

Farmers settled nearby to feed the workmen. Girls and gamblers came to entertain them. Newt's Ford boomed. Quint convinced the railroad that a spur line into town would be profitable. With the grading crews at work, Quint's mill was already starting to turn out sleepers.

Newt's Ford kept growing.

The sun was low at Dutch's back when he ambled his mount across the bridge into town.

The coach house was at his left, overlooking the river. It was a large two-story frame building with a dining room, an office, and a saloon on the ground floor. The hotel rooms took up the second story.

The bank across from the coach house was of red brick. The rest of the buildings lining the wide street were of lumber from Quint Leslie's mill. Some were sturdy and solid, some shoddy behind their false fronts.

The town was installing plank walks. That was another project Quint Leslie had encouraged for his own profit. The walk had been completed on the coach house side of the street. On the other side, it extended just past the Red Rooster Saloon. There, the street was cluttered with heaps of cut planks and stacks of beams from Quint's mill. The banging of hammers rattled back and forth between the false fronts as the work went on.

As he rode into town, Dutch scanned the street sadly. He disliked seeing Newt's Ford grow so hastily and haphazardly. It seemed an ugly scar on the land.

Passing the coach house, he turned into the alley between it and a hardware store. The livery stable and smithy were back off the street, next to the coach yards.

The smith, Tinker Jim, was at his forge cutting nails. He looked up, giving Dutch a nod of greeting.

He was a broad, bandy man, very full through the shoulders and chest, with narrow hips and squat, bowed legs. Dutch thought he looked like a kobold from one of the old tales. Back in Hesse, people said that the kobolds lived inside the mountains, mining and working metals. They said that kobold metal was magic. But Tinker Jim's horseshoes wore thin just as quickly as the ones Dutch forged himself, and the horses wearing them stumbled just as often.

Tinker Jim tugged a big red bandanna from a pocket. He wiped at the sooty sweat on his face with it, looked critically at the big bay gelding Dutch rode, and asked, "You need shoes?"

"No. For the horse, a stall tonight. In the morning, a rig for to hire."

"A rig?"

Dutch nodded. All of the ranch wagons were out on roundup and he didn't own a buggy. He had never needed one before. Now he would have to hire one to drive Hannchen and her chaperone to the ranch in the morning. "A nice rig for two passengers and the driver."

"Got company coming?" Tinker Jim asked curiously.

Dutch nodded again, but he offered no satisfaction for the smith's curiosity. He had told no one except Slim Walker about his bride-to-be. He could trust Slim not to spread gossip. He disliked rumors. He disliked other people nosing into his business.

"A nice rig, huh?" Tinker Jim said thoughtfully. "Let's see now. I've got a runabout that I could let you have cheap. You could squeeze three people into it. Or a buckboard. Or for an extra two bits a day, I could let you have a real nice sprung surrey, got a canvas top on it."

"The surrey. And a good team."

"What time you want them?"

"Early."

"Well, I got some work to do on the Feeleys' cookstove first thing come morning. But I'll send my boy, Jimmy, over. He can get the surrey slicked up and ready for you."

"Obliged." Dutch swung down from the saddle. "The stall for the horse?"

"Box or straight?"

"Box."

Tinker Jim accepted the reins and led the bay to the barn.

Walking stiffly, still aching, Dutch walked back through the alley to the street.

In the long, low shadows cast by the setting sun, the plank layers were packing up their tools. Shops were closing for the night. A man was lighting the lanterns in front of the coach house. Down at the Red Rooster, the lanterns were already glowing, and the sound of loud music was spilling through the swinging doors.

Dutch peered up the road. No sign yet of the coach. It would probably be late, he thought.

Suddenly he was aware of someone coming up close behind him. Wheeling, he found himself facing Sam Steele.

"Howdy, Dutch," Sam said jovially. His voice was husky. His breath smelled of whiskey. His joviality seemed forced.

"Good evening, Sam," Dutch replied, wondering what the town marshal wanted with him. Sam Steele wouldn't go out of his way just to say howdy to Dutch Falke. It had to be a matter of business.

"Buy you a drink?" Sam said.

That meant very important business, Dutch decided. He didn't like the idea of anyone buying his drinks. He didn't want debts, not even such small ones. He said, "I will buy."

Sam smiled a bit. "The Rooster?"

Dutch would have preferred the Concord Saloon. It was a quiet place with no piano and no house girls. But it didn't matter. With a nod, he started for the Red Rooster.

The saloon was already busy. Some of the plank layers went directly there from work. Other workmen were drifting in. Soon men from the lumber mill would arrive. A little later, jacks from the timber crews would come in, and diggers from the coalpits. There would be fights, perhaps injuries, perhaps even death, before the saloon closed.

At the far end of the room, the piano jangled. Girls bunched at one end of the bar eyed Dutch and Sam. When Dutch stopped at the bar to pick up a bottle, one girl approached him. Her smile was stiff, as if it had been painted on. He glared at her. She backed away, looking a little frightened and a little relieved. He wondered if she had heard the gossip about him.

Sam Steele went straight to a table. He was a big man. In his day, he might have been a match for Dutch. But his day was long past. His broad shoulders slumped. His spine bowed with the weight of the belly that thrust out ahead of him. Wattles sagged under his wide jaw. His walk was a shuffle that smeared the sawdust on the saloon floor. Taking the table nearest the door, he dropped into a chair with a heavy grunt, as if the walk had exhausted him.

Dutch carried the bottle and glasses to the table. He filled both glasses. Sam immediately emptied one, sighed, then said, "What brings you into town today, Dutch?"

"Business," Dutch replied tersely. He took a swallow of his drink. Suddenly it occurred to him to wonder how Hannchen would feel about the odor of liquor on his breath.

Gesturing at Dutch's bruised face, Sam said, "It looks like maybe you've had some trouble?"

"Is it to you a concern?"

"Not when it happens outside the town limits. I'm only just a town marshal. Not no sheriff or nothing like that. I got no jurisdiction outside the town. You know that, Dutch."

Dutch nodded, glad of it. He had small use for Sam Steele.

Sam drank again, then went on, "That's what I want you to understand. I'm the only law around here, and I ain't got no jurisdiction outside of town. If there was to be trouble, I couldn't do nothing about it. I mean, not unless it was terrible big trouble, like a range war or some such. If something like that was to happen, then somebody would have to send for a federal marshal to come butt into it, and we'd all have a mess on our hands. You know what I mean?"

Dutch figured that Sam meant there was going to be trouble soon. This was Sam's way of giving a warning. Not a kindly warning to be prepared, but a dark warning not to fight back and make the trouble big enough to interest the federal law.

Sam kept on talking. "I'd sure as hell hate to see some kind of a range war around here. Good folk getting scared and killed and things like that. Dutch, there ain't no need for it. Ain't no reason two men can't settle an argument peaceable between themselves without they go getting rough and throwing lead and bringing a federal officer into it. You know what I mean?"

With a look of mock innocence, Dutch said, "What men do you talk about, Sam?"

"You know what I mean!"

"Me and Quint Leslie?"

Sam filled his glass and emptied it again. He leaned across the table as if what he had to say was in confidence. "Dutch, you know if Quint took a mind, he could stomp you and your whole outfit like bugs on a rock!"

"I do not think so."

"Son, Quint owns damn near everything around here except for your range. You know that, don't you?"

"Is he own you, Sam?"

"Nobody owns Sam Steele!" For a moment there was pride and anger in the marshal's bloated face. But it drained away quickly, leaving the eyes looking hollow and old. Sam's voice dropped to a thin whine. "It's hard for a man when he begins to wear out and he's got nothing to fall back on and no young'uns to look out for him. It gets to where he can't handle the notion of trouble no more. Not like when he was a pup, all full of pepper and vinegar. I can't take no lot of trouble at my age, Dutch."

"*I* am not intend to make trouble."

Sam started to speak. Dutch stopped him with a gesture. The sound of galloping horses had caught Dutch's attention. Not the coach arriving. There was no clatter of wheels and gear. Just the pounding of hoofs. Coming from west of town. From the direction of Falcon range.

The horses were being pushed. Could the riders be some of his men with bad news, Dutch wondered. He leaned toward the window. It had been painted over to above eye level, but the paint was chipped and peeling. He looked out through a bare spot.

The three riders jerking rein in front of the Red Rooster weren't Falcon hands. Dutch recognized the clodhoppers who had beaten him that morning.

Shoving back his chair, he rose. He side-stepped, putting his back to the window, standing close to the door.

Sam eyed him in question. "Dutch, I don't want no trouble —"

Dutch silenced him with a gesture.

Voices sounded outside the door. "Are you sure we ought to do this?"

"Hell, why not?"

"But the money — ?"

"We earned it. Can't we spare a few cents for a round of drinks? Ain't we got a right to some fun once in a while?" The speaker slurred as if he had been doing some heavy drinking already.

"But the folks need —"

"Hell, boy, don't you feel like celebrating that new horse of yourn?"

"No," Stony mumbled as he followed his brothers into the saloon.

The wide batwing hid Dutch from their sight as it swung open. They strode to the bar. The girls looked them over critically and exchanged whispers. One shrugged and started toward them.

Brow wrinkled, eyes puzzled, Sam asked Dutch, "What is it? What's up?"

Dutch gave a shake of his head, suggesting that nothing was wrong. He eased open his clenched fists. Hannchen would be here soon. This was no time for him to meet those three.

Quietly, he sidled through the doorway.

None of the brothers noticed him slip out.

Sam Steele considered a moment, then poured himself another drink.

CHAPTER
THREE

Dutch paused in front of the saloon, alert to the sounds behind him. He hadn't worn his gun belt to town, but there was a twin-barreled derringer in his pocket. He held his hand wrapped around the butt, his thumb on the hammer.

A couple of lumber mill hands walked past him and went into the saloon. No one came out.

Easing his grip on the gun, he stepped down to the hitch rail where the sorrel filly and the two slack-lipped plow horses stood tied. The filly perked its ears and eyed him as he approached it.

Apparently the farmers owned only two saddles. The filly had been rigged out with a gunny sack tied onto its back. Ropes run through the rings of a halter served as reins and bit. There was caked sweat around the edges of the pad and the rope holding it in place.

Poor furnishings for a proud horse, Dutch thought as he untied the filly. He led it across the street and into the alley.

Tinker Jim had banked his fire and was gone. The livery barn was dark. Striking a match, Dutch located a lantern hung on a peg by the doorway. He lit the candle in it, perched it on the anvil, and moved the filly into the light.

Stripping away the rope and sack, he examined the filly's barrel. The sack had done no harm, but the rope holding it had started a gall. When he pried open the horse's mouth, he expected to find the crude rope bit had chafed the tender skin over the bridle bars. To his relief, there was no sign of injury. He was glad he had managed to get the filly back from those clodhoppers before they could do it any serious damage.

From the street, he heard the clatter of the coach. His bride-to-be had finally arrived. But she would have to wait. The filly had to be tended.

He turned it into the stall next to his bay and used the gunny sack to scrub the dried sweat from its back. Hunting up Tinker Jim's store of salves, he chose a brand he trusted and treated the starting gall. When he was done, he gave the filly a good scoop of grain.

The smell of horse and salve was strong on his hands when he snuffed out the candle and returned the lantern to its peg. He stopped at the trough outside the barn door to wash his hands. As he was doing it, the big Concord coach, empty now of its passengers and luggage, rumbled through the alley to the barn behind the station.

So Hannchen was waiting and he was late.

He held his hands up before his face. The scent was still strong on them. Even scrubbing with sand had failed to take the odor off. And there was no more time to waste. Wiping his hands on his kerchief, he hurried into the alley.

As he reached the street, he heard shouting and saw a crowd in front of the Red Rooster. The three farmers were at the hitch rail. A whiskey-slurred voice was wailing, "My horse is gone! Somebody's stole my horse!"

Curious men were coming out of the saloon to see what was happening. Sam Steele stepped out. So did Quint Leslie.

Sam began to question the farmers. As they described the filly to him, one of the onlookers sang out, "I seen it happen! I seen a feller in a black suit take a horse like that off the rail and head over toward — look!"

Dutch had left the alley, heading for the coach office. He glanced back and saw a man at the edge of the crowd aiming a finger at him.

"Stop!" someone shouted.

Another hollered, "Get him! Get him, Sam!"

Sam Steele didn't look happy. He didn't like trouble. But he hitched up his sagging gun belt and dutifully started across the street. The three farmers, obviously drunk, followed him. Much of the crowd trailed along.

The farmer in the lead was Wade. As he neared Dutch he jerked to a halt. His eyes widened. "Good God! It's the Dutchman!"

Stony and Rob stumbled up to Wade's side. Stony started to speak. He stammered and fell silent, staring at Dutch.

"But he's — he's —" Rob began. He, too, cut himself short to stare at Dutch.

"What's this?" Quint Leslie said, coming up by Sam Steele's side. There was an oily slyness in his voice. He cocked a brow as he looked at the farmers. "You say Dutch Falke stole a horse off you?"

Wade nodded, then shook his head. He glanced around at Stony and Rob. "Come on, brothers! We better get!"

"Hold on!" Quint insisted. He was a short broad man with saddle-bowed legs, and a look about him like granite, weathered and worn and hard enough to grind down iron. As usual, he was dressed for the range in faded denims and an old cotton shirt. A Bull tag hung from a pocket of his hide vest, and a revolver hung in the well-worn holster at his side. At a glance, he looked like some bandy ranch hand good for forty-and-found at best. But he carried himself with pride, and there was a tone of command in his voice that made men listen.

The three brothers all looked at him. So did Sam Steele.

"Hold on now, boys," Quint said to the farmers. "You got no call to go shying away from the Dutchman. It don't matter what you might've heard about him. He ain't no different from the rest of us."

A man in the crowd gave a scornful snort. Quint Leslie owned most of the town of Newt's Ford, and Dutch Falke owned a reputation as a killer.

Quint continued, "If Dutch stole your horse, you got the law behind you. And the law's got *me* behind it. If a horse has been stole, the matter's got to be settled. Here and now. Come on over here, Dutch."

Resenting the delay, Dutch walked out into the street to meet him.

Quint spoke to the man who claimed to have seen the filly moved. "This here the feller you saw take a horse off the rail?"

The onlooker eyed Dutch. There was reluctance, perhaps fear, in his face.

"Come on, speak up," Quint insisted, putting the full weight and power of his position into his tone.

"Uh huh," the onlooker admitted.

Quint turned to the farmers. "You say the horse was yours?"

The brothers exchanged glances. Wade looked askance at Sam Steele. Until a moment ago, he and his brothers believed they had killed a man. They thought it would be safe for them to claim the unbranded filly as their own. Now they were confronted. And surrounded. Wade wanted to run, but he could see no direction of escape. He couldn't back down. He would have to stand and bluff.

He nodded in reply.

"What kind of a horse?" Quint asked him.

"Filly. Sorrel filly. Purty little thing."

"Dutch," Quint said. "Did you take a sorrel filly from off the rail?"

Impatiently, Dutch answered, "Yes!"

Quint scowled at him. There was a glint of pleasure behind the scowl. "You mean to say you just up and stole this here boy's horse?"

"The horse I take is mine."

31

Sam Steele shook his head. "I seen you ride in, Dutch. You was on that big bay gelding of yours."

Quint asked the crowd, "Anybody see these three fellers ride in?"

A spectator spoke up. "I did. I seen two of them was on big old plow horses. The other one was on a little sorrel filly. I heeded her particular. She was right handy-looking."

Quint turned again to Sam Steele. "You heard the man, Marshal. What you gonna do about it?"

The question distressed Sam. He considered a moment before he said to Dutch, "You claim this here filly is yours?"

"Yes."

"She got your brand on her?"

Wade snapped, "She ain't got *no* brand on her! A horse without a brand rightfully belongs to the man who puts his saddle on it, don't it?"

Sam nodded.

"The filly is not mustang," Dutch said. "It is the blooded horse. Of such a horse, a man does not mark the hide."

"Then how's a man to know who it belongs to?" Sam grumbled.

"I have the paper."

"Bill of sale?"

"Yes."

Quint interrupted. "Then show it to us."

"I am not carry it with me."

One of the onlookers called, "Where is it?"

"My house."

The three farmers glanced at each other with uncertainty. Their bluff wouldn't hold up against a legal paper.

Quint was obviously enjoying the annoyance to Dutch. He told Sam, "Marshal, you're gonna have to see that bill of sale yourself."

Sam turned to Dutch. "I'm gonna have to see that bill of sale."

"Not now," Dutch told him. "I have business in town. Tomorrow I will bring the paper and show it by you."

"No!" Wade protested. He turned to plead with the onlookers. "He'll just go home and write up a paper of some kind himself and bring it here! That won't prove nothing!"

Dutch sighed with disgust. "I have bill of sale on letterhead by Missouri horse dealer. Is good receipt."

"We got to see it," Quint said.

Sam spoke to Quint. "I can't see no harm in waiting until tomorrow."

The crowd muttered in agreement. Quint didn't argue.

Turning to the farmers, Sam said, "That all right with you?"

"No," Wade grumbled. He looked around, hoping for support. No one spoke up for him. Unwillingly, he nodded. "I reckon."

"Where is the horse now?" Quint asked.

"Tinker Jim's barn," Dutch replied.

"Sam, you'd better make sure that's where she is. Make sure she stays there until you've had a good look at this bill of sale," Quint said.

"I'll put a guard on her."

"You better take a look at her yourself. See to it she's really there."

"Uh huh," Sam grunted. He wasn't eager for the exercise, but Quint Leslie's suggestion was as good as an order. "Come on, Dutch, you want to show her to me?"

Dutch glanced at the coach house where his bride-to-be was waiting for him. Suppressing his anger at the delay, he wheeled and strode toward the alley.

Sam trotted along behind.

Lighting the lantern, Dutch led Sam into the barn. He asked, "Are you believe I steal the horse?"

"No," Sam mumbled. "Not this one."

"You believe I steal some other horse?"

"I don't know. Hell, Dutch, you know how folks tell stories about you. There's some folks that say where there's smoke there must be fire." Sam's tone was curious. He hoped Dutch would confirm or deny the stories.

Dutch knew the tales well enough. He had heard the rumors that he'd begun his ranch with stolen cattle, that his crew was made up of owlhoots wanted by the law in other places, that they kept nesters and strangers off Falcon land with a lynch rope. He gave Sam no reply. Holding up the lantern, he pointed over the stall gate at the filly.

34

Sam took a close look. "Yeah, I reckon that's a sorrel filly all right."

"Enough?"

"Uh huh."

Dutch turned his back on the marshal. Snuffing the candle, he replaced the lantern and walked out of the barn.

When he reached the street, the crowd in front of the Red Rooster had thinned. The two plow horses were gone from the hitch rail. He thought the three farmers didn't care for trouble. By morning, he supposed they would be far away. He put them out of his mind as he went on to the coach house.

The clerk was alone in the office, dozing at the desk. Waking him, Dutch asked about two women passengers from the stagecoach. The clerk remembered them. They had left their luggage in the office. He had a notion they might have gone to the restaurant next door.

Dutch arranged for rooms for them and himself, then went on to the restaurant.

Through the door, he could hear a hum of voices and the clatter of tableware. He stepped inside and scanned the dining room. Most of the tables were occupied by townsfolk enjoying a meal out. In a corner, he spotted two women and a man sharing a table. All three looked dusty and bedraggled. They would be coach passengers, he thought. He could see no others who looked that way.

The woman with her back to him was wearing a dark traveling suit with a short cape, and a feathered bonnet.

He could see only that she was very tall and very slender.

The one with her face toward him was stocky, with a very young, round face. Wisps of straw-colored hair escaped the dark blue bonnet she wore. Her suit was of a blue to match the bonnet, and there was a ruffle of white lace at her throat. The lace drooped limply. The girl looked worn and weary from her long journey. But the tilt of her head was pert as she looked at the man seated beside her.

Dutch was certain she must be Hannchen Gerber. He felt a catch of tension in his throat. As Herr Onkel Heinrich had said, she was very pretty. But she looked terribly young. In a way, her face seemed incomplete, not fully formed. It was the face of a child not yet turned woman.

The man at her side spoke to her. She smiled coyly at whatever he said. Her eyes danced with delight, as if it had been a very flattering compliment.

The man was young and thin, with a very straight back. His jaw was clean-shaven, his brown mustache small and trim. Curly brown hair topped a face that was well tanned, but not weathered in the way of a cowhand's. The suit he wore was neatly tailored. He gestured with his fork as he spoke. The hand holding the fork was very long-fingered and slim. The gesture was sharp, as if the man were tense, high-strung by nature.

As Dutch approached the table, the man looked up. His eyes were pale blue, with a look of deep secrets in them.

36

The tall woman turned to see who was halting at her side. Her face was long and gaunt, all straight lines and flat planes. She was much older than the girl. Her eyes on Dutch were disdainfully questioning, as if he presented an unwanted interruption.

The girl sniffed. Her nose wrinkled at the scents of horse and salve that clung to Dutch. She frowned with revulsion as she glanced at the ugly gash on his forehead.

Embarrassed, angry at the circumstances that had conspired against him, Dutch glared at them. His expression challenged their unspoken criticism. His voice was stiffly harsh. "I am Bartel Falke."

The girl sucked a sharp breath. Her eyes widened in a look that was close to horror. "*Sie sind Herr Falke!*"

"*Nicht sprechen Sie Englisch?*" Dutch snapped at her.

She shrank from the lash of his tone. Dropping her gaze, she gulped, "*Ja.*"

"Then speak it. This is America, not Hesse!"

The young man shoved back his chair. Rising to face Dutch eye to eye, he said, "Mr. Falke, I think your manner is uncalled for!"

Dutch knew that was so. His manner was rude. But all the angers of the day were building into an overwhelming pressure in him. This meeting was far from what it should have been, and the fault was none of his own. But the women judged him at fault. He glowered at the man. "Who are you?"

"James Easton, at your service, sir!" The man's voice snapped like the crack of a whip, as if he offered a challenge to a duel.

The tall woman stood to interrupt before Dutch could speak again. She was almost as tall as Dutch himself. Her accent was English. Her words were sharp and clipped. "Herr Falke, I am Mrs. Claudia Prescott, tutoress and traveling companion to Fräulein Gerber. Mr. Easton was a fellow passenger on the stagecoach. When we found no one here to meet us upon our arrival, he was kind enough to act as our protector."

Hannchen uttered a small, nervous giggle. Dutch darted a dark look at her. She was watching him from under lowered lashes. She suppressed the giggle.

"We hardly expected to be abandoned on the street in this wilderness, Herr Falke, subject to the whims of fate," Claudia Prescott continued. "It was our very good fortune that Mr. Easton was present to aid us in our distress."

"Because I am late by a few minutes, you are in such distress?" Dutch growled at her.

She looked down the length of a long nose at him. "The delay is hardly my only cause for distress, Herr Falke. I was given to understand by your uncle, Herr Heinrich Reiter, that you were a man of station, sir. I had expected the coach to be met by a *gentleman!*"

Everything about Claudia Prescott, her manner, her expression, her tone, seemed calculated to be as insulting as possible.

Dutch's accent thickened with anger. "What *you* are expect is not concern to me. It is for you to make deliver Hannchen Gerber here safe to me. Nothing more!"

"That is hardly correct! It is not my job to *deliver* this poor child to you as if she were some piece of merchant's ware. It is my duty to see to her well-being!"

Hannchen was still watching from under her lashes, but she was no longer struggling not to giggle. Patches of color were rising on her cheeks. A tear formed on a lash. It broke loose, rolling down her face. She snuffled.

Easton took a sidling step toward her, as if to offer protection and comfort. "Mr. Falke, I am afraid you are upsetting Miss Gerber."

Dutch looked at the girl and saw the tears. That disturbed him. He hadn't meant to hurt her. Suddenly his anger melted into a sense of helplessness. It was an unfamiliar feeling. Eager to escape it, he turned again to Claudia Prescott. With a slightly stiff bow, he said, "I have arranged for you and Miss Gerber a room in the hotel. Tomorrow, I will be come to drive you to the ranch. Yes?"

Without awaiting a response, he strode out of the restaurant.

CHAPTER
FOUR

The Concord was a quiet saloon, with no music and no girls. The bar ran the length of one paneled wall. Shaded Rochester lamps over the tables gave off a mellow light. The window onto the street was hung with heavy velour drapes. In the Concord, a man could find a sense of peace and privacy.

When Dutch entered, there were only a few men at the bar. A card game was in progress at the back of the long narrow room. The players were all local businessmen, all solemnly involved in their game. A couple of other tables were taken by townsmen holding serious discussions over their drinks. Voices were held low. Men glanced at Dutch as he walked into the bar, but they were careful to make no show of noticing him.

He stopped at the bar to order a drink and tip the bartender to bring him a meal from the dining room. Taking a table, he sat down with his back to the wall, and sipped slowly at the whiskey while he waited for his food.

This day had gone to hell in a bucket, he thought. He had gotten off to a poor start with his bride-to-be. It seemed to him that was as much the fault of the Prescott woman as it was his own. If she hadn't come at him with her fangs and claws bared, putting him on the defensive, he felt he could have made a decent impression on Hannchen. As it was, he had only succeeded in frightening the girl.

In his letters, Herr Onkel Heinrich had spoken highly of the advantages of taking a very young wife. He had said young girls were like yearling fillies, lively and alert and quick to learn. A man could train one to his own ways. Dutch had meant to approach the girl as he would a green filly, gently calming her fears and winning her trust.

The bartender brought his plate from the dining room. It was heaped high, and the food was good, but Dutch paid small attention to it, eating automatically. His thoughts were all on Hannchen.

He told himself that tomorrow would be different. The women would be rested from their long trip, and he would be rested from this day's problems. They would all start out fresh in the morning. Without James Easton in the way.

He hadn't liked Easton. Something about the man raised his hackles, like the faint scent of a rattlesnake.

He glanced up from his meal as the batwings swung open and Quint Leslie entered the saloon. Pausing just inside the doorway, Quint looked around. His eyes found Dutch and fastened on him.

Dutch was in no mood to be bothered with Quint now. But the rancher looked as if he had important business on his mind.

Dutch met his gaze and lifted a brow in question.

Quint strode over to the table. Giving a curt nod of greeting, he peered at Dutch's bruised face. "You look like you done been drug by your horse."

Dutch said nothing. He waited, fork poised and eyes impatient.

"Anything to do with the trouble out in the street about that filly?" Quint said.

"You call such a small matter *trouble*?" Dutch replied, resenting the question. It was none of Quint's business. He pointedly did not invite Quint to sit down.

Quint stood hunched over the table, his head and jaw thrust forward. His voice rolled like an avalanche of gravel. "You don't like trouble, do you, Dutchman?"

Dutch felt a tightening in his neck and at the hinges of his jaw. He understood there was threat behind Quint's words. Quirking a brow, he said blandly, "Am I going to have trouble?"

Quint eased back a bit as if offering to withdraw his threat. His voice softened. "No need of it, Dutchman. No need for no trouble at all."

Unspeaking, Dutch waited for him to go on.

Quint waved at the bartender and called loudly for whiskey. Several customers scowled at him, disapproving of his shouting in this quiet place. Quint fit far better in the rowdy Red Rooster than in the genteel Concord.

Quint's manner annoyed Dutch. The man seemed determined to damage everything he touched. His presence marred the atmosphere of the Concord. An urge to accept the threat and fight him stirred in Dutch. He told himself he must not let emotion

42

override his sense. Quietly, he said, "Are you want to sit down and discuss it?"

Quint jerked out a chair and dropped into it. He sat heavily, like a man glad to be off aching feet. Dutch knew a lot of cowhands wore their boots too small. It was vanity. He wondered if this crude man who seldom bothered with a bath or a clean shirt was vain about the size of his feet.

The bartender brought a glass and a bottle, and poured for Quint. Quint gestured for him to top off Dutch's drink. Dutch covered the glass with his hand before the bartender could pour. Quint frowned as he realized that Dutch was refusing to accept a drink from him. But he straightened the frown, forcing it into a semblance of a sociable smile as he looked into Dutch's face again. "I ain't an unreasonable man, Dutch. You know that."

"Have I say you are unreasonable?"

Quint shook his head. "You ain't unreasonable either. Leastways, I hope you ain't."

"Has someone say I am?"

"Damn right!" Quint snapped. He caught himself and softened his tone. "Dutchman, you been stubborn as an Arkansas jack rabbit when I try to talk business with you."

Dutch shrugged. "When first you come here, we make agreement. You will stay on this side of river and I will keep my range on other side."

"Things have changed since we made that agreement."

"Yes."

"The situation's different now. I explained that to you, Dutch. I told you I'm crowded. I'm running as much beef as my grass will carry. If I'm gonna expand my herd, I got to have more grass."

Dutch knew that whether Quint meant to put more beef on the range or not, he would still have to find new grass. His land was already overgrazed. Quint had timbered out much of the range and stripped more for coal. Spring rains and runoff had eroded away a lot of topsoil. Land that should have been lush with grass was now barren and useless. Quint had destroyed it. So now he felt crowded, in need of new land.

"What is that to me?" Dutch said.

"You got plenty of grass," Quint growled. "You never ran half the stock your land can carry. You got a damn sight more good grass over on your side of the river than you use."

Dutch nodded in agreement. He ran enough stock to make enough money to live comfortably and pay his crew decently. He didn't need more than that.

"All I want is to lease graze off you," Quint said. "I ain't trying to take it from you. I ain't asking something for nothing. I just want to lease some of that grass you ain't using to put my own beef on. It won't cost you nothing. It'll only put money in your pocket. What the hell you got against that, Dutchman?"

Dutch snorted softly through his nose. He could hardly make Quint understand that a part of it was the way Quint kept addressing him as "Dutchman", as if he didn't warrant the respect of a name. Nor could he possibly make Quint see the land and the forests and

44

the grass as anything more than a commodity to be sold for profit.

He said, "I have see you at work, Quint. I have see you move in your cattle and take over the range by this side of the river. I have see you run nesters off your range —"

"*I* never hanged none of them!" Quint snapped.

Dutch's eyes narrowed slightly, but he went on as if he hadn't been interrupted. "I have see you make this town your own —"

"Wasn't no town here at all when I came. I built this town!"

"I could be lease you land now. I could be let you drive a herd across the river. I could be let you build on my range the line camps. There would be no trouble —"

"Damn right there wouldn't!"

"Not now perhaps. But in a year or two, then what? When you are want to expand again your herd, then what? How long would be, Quint, before you decide you need *all* of Falcon grass? How long before you want to cut from Falcon range the timber? How long before you find coal to take from under the ground? How long before there is trouble?"

"Dammit, Dutchman!" Quint slammed a fist down on the table. The glasses tottered at the jolt. Customers glared at the noise. Quint sucked a breath, reining in his anger. He eyed Dutch. "I'm giving you this one last chance, Dutchman. Most of that land ain't yours by right of law nohow. I got as much right to use it as you do. You either lease me what I want, all nice and decent and clean, or I'll take what I need, and you can go to hell with your damned Falcon brand!"

"You say the land is not mine by the law. Are you want to put the question to the law?" Dutch said coolly.

Quint edged back a bit. "Hell, I don't want no damned federal marshals poking around, and neither do you."

"You are not want the law to know what use you make of the land you have now?"

Obviously Quint didn't. Drawing himself up with a scowl, he replied, "Where I come from, a man does his own fighting. He don't pussyfoot off to somebody else to do it for him."

Dutch's mouth quirked. "Are you want to fight, Quint? Man to man? With fists or guns in the street? Now?"

Quint glanced at the broadness of Dutch's shoulders. He knew the quickness of Dutch's hand. Slowly, he drawled, "I do my fighting with my brains."

"So?"

"Look here, Dutchman, you don't want no mess of trouble now. Not with that pretty little bride of yourn fresh arrived in town. You don't want to go giving her a gravestone for a wedding present, do you?"

Dutch felt a sudden chill along his spine. And sudden anger that this man should know of his plans to marry. How did Quint Leslie know? Dutch had told no one but Slim Walker. He trusted Slim.

"Tell you what," Quint was saying. "S'pose we make a deal."

"Deal?"

46

"A bet. I'll bet you I can bed a thousand head of beef on some of Falcon's best grass within a week's time. If you figure you can keep me from doing it, back your hand. If I do it, you'll move on somewheres else and leave all the range around here to me. If you can keep me off the land for a week, I'll move out and you can take over my land."

That was one hell of a proposal. It startled Dutch. He eyed Quint as he considered. What was in it for the rancher? Well, it would put a deadline on the fighting. It would keep Falcon from bringing in hired guns. With Newt's Ford booming, Dutch wouldn't be able to hire good men around town to help. He would have to rely on the men he already had.

The Falcon crew was in the last week of roundup. Perhaps Quint thought the men would be too work-worn and weary to fight. Perhaps he thought they would not be willing. If so, he was wrong. Dutch knew his men. Every one of them was hard and strong, and loyal to the brand. Weary or not, they would fight for Falcon.

Quint offered no choice except fight or surrender. By the terms of the bet, the war would not last more than a week. Win or lose, that would be it.

Dutch disliked pulling the men off roundup. He knew the longer they were away from the work, the more of it would have to be done over when they returned. He said, "Not this week. Later."

"Now or nothing!" Quint replied. "I'll have my beef on your grass by the end of this week, no matter what.

You can drag it out into a long war if you want, or you can take my bet and pull out clean when I've won. It's up to you, Dutchman!"

He was too damned sure of himself, Dutch thought. As if he knew he was holding aces. But it seemed nothing was to be lost through accepting the bet. And much might be gained. Perhaps these mountains could be rid of Quint Leslie for good.

"A day, then," Dutch suggested. "You give me a day for to take the women to the ranch and see they be settled comfortably. Yes?"

"Sure!" Quint agreed with a grin. On his face, the expression looked misshapen and ugly enough to send another icy chill down Dutch's spine.

The touch of Quint's hand as they shook on it left Dutch's palm feeling clammy. He wiped it on his napkin as he watched Quint stride confidently out of the saloon.

What did Quint have up his sleeve, he wondered.

Dutch awoke with a sense of foreboding. As he dressed, he tried to force away the dark thoughts of Quint Leslie. Today he must befriend Hannchen Gerber. He wanted to learn what kind of woman Herr Onkel Heinrich had sent him for a wife. Today he must make an effort to give her a good impression of himself.

The light of dawn spilled through his window into the bedroom, but the hallway was still dark as he made his way to the door of the room he had rented for the women.

Several long moments passed before a gruff, sleep-heavy voice answered his knock. Claudia Prescott called through the closed door, "What is it?"

"Bartel Falke. I am come to take you to the ranch."

"What! Now? Why, it's not daylight yet!" she snapped.

He realized that the women must have been asleep when he knocked. He told himself he should have known that after their long, wearisome journey they would be late to rise. But he hadn't thought about that, so he had made a mistake, and another day was off to a bad start.

He asked, "Will you be ready soon?"

"We can hardly prepare ourselves instantly!"

"Then I will be wait for you by the dining room. Yes?"

"Yes," she replied, sounding thoroughly disgruntled.

With a sigh, Dutch headed downstairs.

He found that the dining room wasn't open yet. The waiter girls were just spreading fresh cloths on the tables. One told him they wouldn't begin to serve for another half hour.

As he turned away, he was thinking of the cowhands on the range. They would have eaten breakfast before the sun rose. At this hour, they would be hard at work.

He supposed that Hannchen and the Prescott woman would be down by the time the dining room opened. Meanwhile, he could collect the surrey.

Behind the coach house, hostlers were currying the horses that would take the big Concord coach on to the next station. At the livery stable, there was no sign of activity at all.

Dutch helped himself to the lantern. As he stepped into the barn, he heard a crackling of dry straw. Instinctively, his hand started for his thigh, for the gun he usually wore there. But today he wasn't wearing it.

A head appeared above a stall gate. And with it a horse pistol. It was one of the huge Dragoon cap-and-ball pistols that had been carried a lot during the War Between the States. The muzzle was monstrous, the bore a gaping black hole. It pointed directly at Dutch. Over it, a pair of bleary eyes peered at him.

A fuzzy voice, raw from long years of use and a lot of hard whiskey, asked pleasantly, "You come horse thieving, Dutch?"

Dutch spread his hands, showing that he held only the lantern. He gave a grin to the old man behind the big pistol. "Not horse thieving, Bark. I am come to get my saddle horse and the surrey I have hire yesterday. You are here to guard the filly, yes?"

The head nodded. Bark was one of the loafers who warmed the bench in front of the Red Rooster during the day and a chair inside during the evenings. He carried his age and whiskey well. The town paid him to swamp out the marshal's office and the jail cells once a week. Sam Steele occasionally hired him on for odd jobs.

Squinting at Dutch over the gun, Bark said, "It's a good thing he did. Somebody tried to sneak in here last night. Was it you, Dutch?"

50

"No. I have sleep all night. You did not see who it was?"

Bark shook his head. "I scared 'em off before I could get a look at 'em."

Probably the farmers, Dutch thought.

Bark went on, "Sam says I can't let nobody take that there filly away until he says so."

"She is not the horse I am come for," Dutch told him. "I come for the bay in the next stall."

"You sure?"

"Yes."

"I reckon it ain't none of my business if you take him. Sam didn't say nothing about no horses but the filly."

Glancing around, Dutch asked, "Tinker Jim is not here yet?"

Bark shook his head. "Ain't showed up. Slugabeds! That's what all these young pups is these days! Just slugabeds! When I was young, I'd 've had the cows milked and the eggs collected and half a dozen acres plowed by now. In the war, we didn't sleep till noon. I can tell you that! You lay abed past first light in them days, and a sharpshooter would see to it you didn't wake up no more never!"

"What about the son?"

"Son? You mean Tinker Jim's boy? What about him?"

"You are not see him yet?"

"No. I ain't seen nobody but you. They're all a bunch of slugabeds!"

Dutch shrugged and went on to the bay's stall. The horse thrust out its head, eying him curiously. Bark went on telling some story of the war as Dutch grained the bay.

"Halloo!" a voice called from outside the barn. It was young, high-pitched, and cautious. "Somebody inside there?"

"Jimmy?" Bark hollered back. "That you?"

"Uh huh. Who's that? Bark?"

"It ain't Stonewall Jackson!"

The boy came into the barn. He was thin-chested and gangly, already a head taller than his father, and still growing. "What you doing here, Bark? Who's that with you?" Giggling, he added, "Miss Lucy?"

"You'd be surprised, boy," Bark cackled back at him.

Dutch stepped out of the bay's stall, showing himself to Tinker Jim's son.

"Oh, jeez!" Jimmy grunted at the sight of him. "The team!"

"What about the team?"

"They're still down to pasture. Pa told me to fetch them in this morning for you, only I sort of forgot."

"Then go get them."

Jimmy drew a deep breath, then sighed sadly. "All right. But it'll take me a while."

"Hurry."

"Yes sir!"

As Jimmy raced away, Bark commented to Dutch, "These here young'uns nowadays ain't good for much. They always got other things on their minds, never keep put to the business at hand. It was different when I was a boy. If you didn't keep your mind to business, you didn't keep your scalp to your head. I recollect when my folks brung me West. The plains was thick with Sioux in them days, Dutch. You can't hardly imagine. Sioux and buffalo! Nothing but miles and miles of buffalo! You never seen such a sight!"

Half-listening to the old man ramble, Dutch tended the bay. He had the horse saddled and was waiting idly when Jimmy finally returned with the team.

Once the surrey was ready, Dutch hitched the bay behind it and drove through the alley to the street. The dining room was open and busy. Leaving the surrey at the rail in front of the coach house, he went to the dining room door and looked through the glass.

The women were inside, having breakfast. James Easton was with them. Easton said something and all three laughed.

Suddenly Dutch was angry. Too angry to be civil. But he didn't want another argument with the Prescott woman. If he spoke to her before he had his temper under control, he knew there would be an ugly scene.

Wheeling away from the door, he began to walk.

He *had* to keep himself under control today and make a decent impression on the woman he expected to marry. He had to be polite and hold his tongue when the Prescott woman irked him. He had to show Hannchen Gerber he was a decent man, suitable for a husband.

He wasn't at all sure he could handle himself with Easton present. For some reason, just the sight of Easton struck sparks in him. Who the hell was Easton? he wondered.

Walking was good. It calmed a man's nerves and let him think. Dutch's long, swinging stride took him out past the edge of town into the grassland, then back again. By the time he returned, he had worn off much of the tension. He felt capable of facing the women, perhaps even Easton. But they were gone from the dining room when he arrived.

He found the three of them chatting together in the hotel lobby. Evidently they were enjoying one another's company very much.

Drawing a deep breath, Dutch resolutely walked in.

There was a smile on Claudia Prescott's wide, thin mouth when she looked up. Recognizing Dutch, she let the smile slip away. Her mouth tightened grimly. "You are late again, Mr. Falke!"

Hannchen turned her wide eyes to Dutch, looking as if she expected him to start ranting at her. In a small voice, she murmured, "Good morning, Mr. Falke."

Rising, Easton bobbed his head to Dutch. It was a nod of greeting, but hardly of welcome. He seemed to reciprocate Dutch's instinctive dislike.

They all acted as if he were some kind of ogre, Dutch thought. The anger burned in his gullet again. Stiffly, he asked, "You are ready to go now?"

"We have been ready for quite some time," Claudia Prescott replied.

"This is yours?" Dutch indicated the luggage piled beside the door. There were three trunks and nearly a dozen small cases. To him, it seemed like a heavy load for just two people.

54

"Yes," Claudia sighed wearily, sounding as if she had been inconvenienced beyond human endurance. "We have been forced to travel very lightly."

The office clerk was watching and listening. A small smile of amusement twisted his mouth. As Dutch scowled at him, the smile disappeared.

"Have a man bring to the surrey these things," Dutch snapped at him.

"Yes sir!"

Wheeling away from the women, Dutch strode out to the walk. He knew he was making mistakes again, and adding to the poor impression of himself that he had already given Hannchen. But the anger in him was overwhelming.

He told himself it would be better once they were at the ranch, away from town and from James Easton.

CHAPTER
FIVE

There was too much luggage. It filled the back of the surrey and had to be lashed in place with rope. No room was left for a passenger in the back. Both women had to squeeze onto the front bench with Dutch.

They both sat stiffly gazing ahead in silence as he drove the surrey out of town. Claudia Prescott was in the middle, like an icy barrier to keep him from Hannchen.

Watching the road ahead, he held his mouth grimly closed. The silence was uncomfortable, but he didn't intend to be the one who broke it. He felt as if he were in battle with the Prescott woman and the first one to speak would be conceding to the other. He did not mean to let her beat him.

He allowed to himself that all his fine plans for this day had gone sour. He had failed to make the good impression on Hannchen that he had hoped for. Would he ever be able to befriend the girl, he wondered. Perhaps she would always look at him with fear in her wide eyes. That would be worse than no wife at all.

He considered putting her onto the next coach East with passage money home to Hesse. He could send her back to Herr Onkel Heinrich with apologies. But being rejected that way would disgrace Hannchen and insult Herr Onkel. And it would sure as hell set the folks around Newt's Ford talking.

Dutch felt he could put up with the rumors and slanders, but he couldn't bring himself to hurt Herr Onkel. He would have to work something out with Hannchen somehow. He didn't think he could do it while the Englishwoman was ready to stand like a granite rock between them. Perhaps things would be better once the wedding was over and Claudia Prescott was gone.

The coach road through Newt's Ford was good. The fork off to Falcon headquarters was another matter. It was just adequate for supply wagons. As he turned the surrey onto it, Dutch kept the team at a trot. The wheels jounced over the ruts and rocks and through shallow streams. The surrey bobbed and swayed.

Both women had to hold on to their hats. At times Hannchen let out small squeaks. Claudia Prescott kept gazing straight ahead. Dutch was determined to force her into breaking the silence. He wanted her to beg him to ease the pace. Slapping the horses' rumps with the reins, he speeded up the trot.

Suddenly something clattered on the road behind them. Claudia looked back. She broke the silence with a demanding shout. "Stop!"

It was not the victory Dutch had hoped for.

He brought the team to a halt, gave the reins a wrap around the whip socket, and jumped to the ground. At the back of the surrey, he found that one of the traveling cases had slipped free of the lashing rope and was gone. When he looked along the road, he could see no sign of it.

Walking back, he discovered that it had gone traveling. Bouncing over the low brush at the side of the road, it had crushed a path through the fresh spring growth as it rolled down the steepening slope, then plunged over an abrupt drop. It lay at the bottom of an embankment, spilling bright blue fabric from its open mouth.

Claudia and Hannchen followed him from the surrey. Spotting her case, Hannchen squealed, *"Ach! Mein Reisekoffer!"*

"That was very careless," Claudia said sharply to Dutch. She cocked a brow at him. "I trust the case can be recovered!"

He was tempted to say to hell with it.

Hannchen asked hopefully, *"Bitte?"*

"Speak English!" he snapped at her.

She blinked as she nodded. Dampness began to glisten in her eyes.

Dutch darted a scowl at Claudia. It was the Englishwoman's fault he had spoken so harshly to Hannchen. The Englishwoman kept him on edge, with his temper barely under control. He felt like strangling her.

He managed to keep his anger out of his voice as he spoke to Hannchen. "It is necessary you be learn always to speak English here. You must learn to be think in English. You are a stranger here, and strange to the people here. If you wish to learn to live by them and deal by them, you must speak their language and keep their ways. If you do not, you will always be a stranger here. Understand?"

She nodded.

Claudia growled, "Are we going to stand here all day, Mr. Falke?"

He told himself it would be foolish to abandon the traveling case. And unfair to Hannchen. It certainly wouldn't help him win her confidence. With a sigh, he started back to the surrey.

"Mr. Falke!" Claudia demanded.

"I will get the case," he said.

He had used the catch rope from his saddle to lash the luggage onto the surrey. To untie the rope, he had to unload some of the cases. The women stood watching. Neither offered to help.

There was no convenient place to anchor the rope on the top of the embankment. He had to tie it to a large bush at a distance from the brink. The ledge below, where the case rested, was level and wide enough for him to walk easily on it, but the face of the embankment was a sheer drop. Hanging on to the rope, he lowered himself over the edge and worked his way hand over hand down the rope. He dropped the last few feet to the ledge.

"Look around! Be certain nothing fell out of the case!" Claudia shouted at him, as if he hadn't sense enough to know that for himself. He had already spotted a piece of clothing caught on a bush. He got it, tucked it into the case, then closed the latches.

"Are you certain you have everything?" Claudia called as he tied the case onto the rope.

He didn't bother to reply, but shouted at her, "Pull it up!"

"What?"

"Pull up the case and off the rope take it," he instructed impatiently. "Then throw back down by me the rope!"

"*Ja! Ja!*" Hannchen gasped, frightened by his tone. She jumped to obey him. As she grabbed for the rope, her toe caught in the hem of her skirt.

Dutch saw her wavering on the brink of the embankment. Clods of earth tumbled from under her feet. She shrieked as the ground gave way beneath her. Skirts billowing, she plunged toward him.

He flung out his arms, hoping to break the force of her fall. Her body slammed into him. His legs buckled. Both of them went to the ground in a tangle of her skirts.

His arms enclosed her protectively. Anxiously, he asked, "*Sind Sie* — are you all right?"

It took her a long moment to get her breath and reply. When she did, her voice was a thin quaver. "*Ja, ich* — I think I be."

Then suddenly she began squirming in his arms, trying to break free of them. He released her. She scrambled to her feet. Clutching her skirts, she backed away from him. Tears began to roll down her cheeks.

Dutch pressed his right hand to the ground to brace himself, and discovered a shock of pain in his shoulder. With a grunt, he shifted his weight and hauled himself up without putting pressure on the shoulder. He held his left hand toward Hannchen.

She started like a shy horse.

"I am not going to hurt you," he said.

From above, Claudia was screaming, "Hannchen! Hannchen, dear! Are you hurt? Are you injured, child?"

Hannchen didn't answer. Her attention was all on Dutch. She seemed to think he would give her some terrible punishment for falling from the embankment.

He replied to Claudia, "She is all right!"

"Are you certain?" The Englishwoman sounded unwilling to trust his opinion.

Grunting to himself with disgust, he walked over to the dangling end of the rope. He tugged it with his right hand. Pain lashed through his shoulder.

The rope was strong enough to bear the weight of the two of them, but his shoulder wasn't. He could never haul himself up it while carrying Hannchen on his back.

He called to Claudia, "You will from the surrey bring my saddle horse."

"What!"

"My horse! Get it! Bring it to where you are stand now."

"No!" She sounded appalled at the idea.

"Bring the horse!" he insisted.

"I don't — I — I couldn't!"

He was afraid he was just wasting his breath arguing with the Englishwoman. Turning to Hannchen, he said, "You are wait here. I go up to do some things, then I put down for you the rope. Yes?"

Unspeaking, she stared at him. The tears streamed from her eyes.

He took hold of the rope.

"*Nein! Nein!*" she screamed, lunging at him. As she grabbed him, she pleaded in German for him not to leave her there.

He realized she was afraid that he meant to abandon her. Facing her, he put his hands on her arms. This time, he spoke to her in German.

"Hannchen, I will not leave you here. Understand? I must go up and prepare the rope for you. Then I will come back down and get you. Yes?"

She seemed doubtful, but when he took hold of the rope again, she didn't try to hang on to him. Slowly, he began to haul himself up.

It wasn't easy. Every time his right arm took his weight, the pain lanced through his shoulder. Teeth clenched, he kept going. It seemed a damned long way to the top. When he finally pulled himself over the edge, he had to lie still a moment to let the pain ease.

Claudia hurried to him. She ranted, "You left that poor frightened child down there all alone!"

He felt like stopping her words with his fist. But that was not done. Catching breath, he got to his feet and started for the surrey.

Still ranting, Claudia followed him.

He untied the bay from the surrey. The horse wasn't a roper, but it didn't need to be. It simply had to obey. He led it back to the top of the embankment and turned it with its rump to the brink.

Taking the end of the rope from the bush, he tied it onto the saddle horse. Then he walked the horse a step forward.

"What are you doing?" Claudia demanded.

"Come here," he said to her.

She hesitated.

"Come here!"

"I — horses — they frighten me," she stammered.

So the granite-hard Englishwoman had her flaws after all, he thought. But this was a damned inconvenient one. She would have to overcome it.

Fighting his anger and disgust, he kept his voice level. "Will you be leave Miss Gerber down there?"

She shook her head.

"She is be frightened. I think she cannot take care of herself." As he spoke, he wondered how a woman who couldn't take care of herself could survive in this wild land. "I must go down for her. You must bring us up."

Eying him suspiciously, Claudia asked, "How?"

"You see what I do?" He backed the horse to the brink, then walked it forward again. "This is all. You make walk the horse. The rope comes up. Yes?"

Again, Claudia shook her head. "I cannot handle a horse!"

"You must. Or I must go get other help. Will you be leave Miss Gerber to wait while I am riding for help?"

Claudia looked at the ledge. She twined her fingers, twisting them tightly with concern. "The poor child! She must be — she —"

"Come," Dutch said firmly. "Take the horse."

Slowly, Claudia approached the horse's head. Her hand trembled as she accepted the reins from Dutch.

The horse stood obediently waiting. Claudia stayed as far from it as she could while holding the bridle.

Dutch told her, "When I am call out, you walk him forward very slowly. Miss Gerber will be on the rope. Understand?"

She nodded.

He lowered himself down the rope hand over hand. It would have been easier to put a foot in the loop and ride it down, with the horse backing, doing the work, but he didn't trust Claudia to handle the animal any more than was absolutely necessary. He disliked trusting her to help at all.

The pain in his shoulder was worse. Each time his right arm took his weight, he felt as if he were about to lose his grip. Suddenly he did. His finger refused to hold and he was falling.

He crumpled as he hit the ground, absorbing the impact the way he would if he were thrown from a bronc. Lying still, face down, he caught breath and collected himself.

He was aware of Hannchen hurrying to his side. She bent over him. Her voice was small and fearful. "*Herr Falke, sind* — are you be dead?"

"No." He sat up and looked at her.

"*Ich* — I was afraid —" Her chin quivered as she spoke. She looked down, avoiding his eyes. "I was think you do not — I was think you be leave me here. You are not be liking me."

"Do you like me?" he asked.

She peeked at him from under her lashes. "I be afraid."

"Of me?"

"*Ja.*"

64

"Is wrong. I do not mean to frighten you. I do not mean to harm you. For us, will be better when the Englishwoman is gone."

"She is not be liking you," Hannchen muttered.

He nodded. That was obvious.

"She is not like anyone in this country, I think," Hannchen went on. "Once her family is have much money in this country. Then there is war to make free from England and her family is be forced to leave their land and money here and go back to England very poor. Now she is angry. She does not like that you are come here poor and become much rich with land and money, and she has none."

"Then why does she come here with you?"

"She is be paid. For a long time now, she is be teach me to speak good the English. When I am be coming from Hesse, must be a woman to come by me and make watch over me. She is paid to bring to you me, but she is not be liking to come. Always she is tell me I am not be liking in America. I think before she is meet you, she is already be not liking you."

"A lot of people do not like me. It is nothing to me," he said. "But you — it is not good if you do not like me. Perhaps you will try."

"I will try." Her voice was small and not very confident.

"Come." He held a hand to her. She took it reluctantly. He led her to the rope and pointed at the dangling loop. It hung above her eye level.

"You are to put there your foot," he told her. "You are stand in the loop and hold on to the rope, yes?

Above, the horse pulls. The loop rises. You ride up by it. Understand?"

Frowning at the high loop, she asked, "How I am put into that my foot? It is too much above!"

"I will lift you."

"So high?"

"On my shoulders." He looked thoughtfully at her, trying to anticipate any difficulties she might encounter. "I think with your skirts can be some trouble."

She glanced down at her mass of skirts. There was dirt on them. She brushed at it.

"You must take them off," he told her.

"*Nein!*" she squeaked.

"Is necessary."

Hesitantly, she asked, "We are be married soon?"

"As soon as can be arranged."

"You must be turn away. Not look, please!"

"I be have to look when I am lift you up."

She thought about that. Slowly she admitted, "Is so."

Taking a deep breath, she began to strip her outer skirt. She bared layers of petticoats trimmed with lace. Her face burned red as she untied the tape holding the top petticoat and dropped it. She avoided Dutch's eyes as she went on untying and dropping petticoats until she had let six of them fall. There was still another to be undone.

"So many?" Dutch said.

At that, she darted an askance look at him and made a small sound that might have been a suppressed giggle.

Then she let the last petticoat fall. Under it, she was wearing pantalets that covered her to the knees and white stockings that disappeared under the pantalets. They hid her skin, but not her shape.

Watching her, he admired the soft, well-rounded body she revealed. It would be a pleasure to hold such a body close. But a man did not spend all his life in bed. He wanted more from a wife than just an attractive body.

"Now?" she asked.

"You must climb to sit on my shoulders," he said, hunkering before her.

As she got herself into position, she giggled. "When I was girl*chen*, the father is be give me rides so."

Dutch grunted in reply. He told her, "Hold on. Reach the rope when you can, yes?"

As he stood up, pain shot through his shoulder. Hannchen gripped his hair, hanging on. Once he was on his feet, standing steady, she eased the grip.

"Can you reach now the rope?" he asked.

"*Ja* — yes, I am have it!"

"Can you get into the loop the foot?"

"I think — *nein* — *ach*, I cannot! I — wait!" She squirmed on his back, sending another shock of pain through his shoulder. As he winced, she asked, "I hurt you?"

"No."

"I am be — there! I am in the rope the foot!"

"Can you stand on it?"

"*Bitte?* Uh — I — yes!"

He felt her shifting, then easing from his back. Carefully, he twisted from under her. She hung on the end of the rope. He said, "Ready?"

"Ja — yes. I hold tight."

Stepping back, he shouted, "Now, Mrs. Prescott! Lead forward the horse now! Slow!"

Claudia obeyed. The rope began to slide up over the edge of the embankment. Hannchen rose at the end of it.

At last she reached the top and Dutch shouted for Claudia to stop the horse. He added that she must stay with it, holding on to the bridle, and not let it go.

Hannchen stopped moving upward. Grabbing at the brink, she squirmed and kicked and finally disappeared from his sight over the edge.

A sudden horrified shriek sounded from above.

"What is? What happens?" Dutch shouted.

There was no reply.

He called again.

Still no answer.

He glanced around anxiously, looking for some way to get up the slope without help. He could see none.

At last Claudia Prescott appeared at the brink above him. Her face was a thunderhead of anger. She began spitting words at him like strikes of lightning. "You beast! You foul vicious animal!"

"Was?" he grunted in astonishment.

She kept on screaming at him.

After several tries, he realized his attempts to get a sensible reply from her were useless. She just wouldn't listen to him.

"Fräulein Gerber!" he shouted. "Fräulein Gerber, *kommen Sie hier! Was ist?*"

Obediently, Hannchen stepped to Claudia's side. She was crying. With anguish, she said, "Herr Falke! *Ich bin — Sie — ach — !*"

Claudia cut her short by wheeling and jerking her back from the brink.

Dutch could no longer see either of them, but he could hear Claudia telling the girl to go get some clothes on immediately before someone happened to pass by and saw her.

Standing on the ledge with no way up, he wished that someone would happen to pass by. He needed help up the embankment, and he was sick of trying to cope with Claudia Prescott. But it was unlikely that anyone would happen to be riding the ranch road.

He waited.

Claudia reappeared. She set in to lashing at him with her sharp tongue again.

He tried to outshout her. "Back up the horse! To me lower now the rope!"

She paid no attention to his orders. She just kept screaming at him.

He sighed wearily, wondering how long she would keep it up.

Finally Hannchen returned to the brink. Her face was still red and tear-stained, but she was no longer sobbing. He called to her in German, asking if she could back the horse and let the rope down to him.

She left his sight. Then the rope began to snake down the face of the embankment. It was barely within his reach when she called to him that the horse could go no closer to the edge without danger of backing off.

"Is enough," he replied, grabbing the loop with his left hand. Bracing against it, he caught a scant foothold on the rocky face of the embankment and hauled himself up enough to secure his grip.

When he called for Hannchen to lead the horse forward slowly, she obeyed him.

Riding the loop up, he reached the brink and dragged himself over it. Immediately Claudia began pouring her wrath out at him.

He got to his feet. Squaring his aching shoulders, he glared at her. Quietly, in a voice as cold as the buzz of a snake's rattles, he said, "Shut up."

Her mouth snapped closed.

Hannchen made a small strangling sound, as if she were trying to swallow a giggle and had choked on it.

Dutch saw that she was dressed again, and he understood the reason for Claudia's outburst of anger. The Englishwoman was upset because he'd had the girl bare herself to the bottom layer of her clothing before him.

"Hell," he grunted to himself.

Collecting herself, Claudia started again. This time she was not so loud and violent. Her voice was grim. "Mr. Falke, what has occurred here is appalling! Absolutely appalling! It is imperative now that the wedding take place as quickly as possible!"

"Yes," he agreed, thinking that the sooner he and Hannchen were married, the sooner he could send the chaperone on her way. He'd had more than enough of Claudia Prescott.

Wondering how Herr Onkel Heinrich could have chosen to send such a woman in the first place, he took the horse from Hannchen and led it back to the surrey.

CHAPTER
SIX

As Dutch reined the team to a halt in front of the ranch house, he frowned at the door.

He had left it latched against wandering animals that might try to raid his larder. The latch string had been out, in case someone from the crew returned in his absence, or someone passing by needed food and shelter. But he had definitely left the door latched. Now it was slightly ajar.

He told himself that most likely he'd had some unexpected company while he was away. Some drifter who had failed to give the door a good tug when he left, or who might still be inside. But Quint Leslie's threats were fresh in his mind, and he didn't intend taking any chances.

"Wait here," he told the women as he stepped down from the surrey. Drawing the little derringer from his pocket, he walked softly to the door. He held the gun ready as he slammed the door open and jumped aside.

Silence.

Cautiously, he looked into the house. And sucked a surprised breath.

The living room was a shambles. Books had been pulled from the shelves and flung heedlessly on the floor. Chairs and tables were overturned. The curios that had accumulated on the mantel had been swept to the floor.

Only one piece of furniture was upright in its place. That was a lamp table. The lamp sitting on it was now missing its chimney.

"Hello!" Dutch called.

His voice rang unanswered.

Gun in hand, he stepped inside. From the direction of the kitchen, he heard a faint scraping sound. Noiselessly, he headed over to the closed kitchen door.

Something moved behind him.

With the thought that he had been lured into a trap and was caught between two enemies, he wheeled. The derringer was leveled, the hammer back, his finger firm on the trigger.

He grunted a curse as he saw Claudia Prescott framed in the doorway. Behind her, Hannchen stood on tiptoe, peering over her shoulder. Claudia gave a start as the gun pointed toward her. A small sharp gasp escaped her tight mouth.

Hannchen squealed.

The gun did not completely unnerve Claudia. Collecting herself, she scowled at it. "Is that thing necessary, Mr. Falke?"

Dutch glowered at her, gesturing for silence. He turned back to the kitchen door and gave it a shove.

For an instant, he was looking directly into a pair of bright brown eyes.

A woman stood in the kitchen, with her back to the outside door and her hand on the latch. For that brief instant she seemed frozen, gazing into Dutch's eyes like a jack-lit doe staring at a lantern. Then her hand tugged the latch and she twisted out through the doorway. She slammed the door shut behind her as Dutch lunged into the kitchen.

Reaching the door, he flung it open. She was well into the yard, running for the woods. She had her ragged skirts caught up in both hands. Her bare feet and slim ankles flashed as she ran.

"Stop!" Dutch shouted, pointing the gun at her.

She didn't even glance back.

Nosing the gun up, well away from her, he shouted once more, then pulled the trigger.

She winced at the sound of the shot. As she looked around, she almost stumbled. But she caught her balance and ran on.

She was as fleet as a doe. Dutch knew he couldn't catch up by running after her. Lowering the gun, he watched her disappear into the trees.

"What is it, Mr. Falke?" Claudia called from the living room. "What are you shooting at? A bear?"

"Red Indians?" Hannchen gasped.

Dutch closed the outside door and returned to the living room. Hannchen was hovering behind Claudia as if for protection. Breathlessly, she asked Dutch, "Is wild red Indians, Mr. Falke? Is be they come back? Is be they cut off my hair? Please?"

Sharply, Claudia corrected her. "*Will* they come back? *Will* they cut off my hair?"

"*Will* they?" Hannchen said, her voice quavering. Her eyes pleaded with Dutch for reassurance.

74

"No," he told her. "There are not wild Indians in these mountains now. They are all far away on government reservations where soldiers watch them. Is no need to fear Indians."

"You be certain?"

He nodded.

"Then what is?" She gestured at the kitchen.

"Intruder. Perhaps robber." He shoved the derringer back into his pocket and turned to the lamp without a chimney. Broken glass lay on the floor next to the table. Not scattered shards but a little heap of it, as if someone had been sweeping it up. That made no sense.

Frowning, he scanned the room. There was a gun rack on the wall next to the front door. He'd had half a dozen long guns in it. Two rifles and a shotgun were missing now.

But the woman in the kitchen had been empty-handed.

He decided this definitely was not Quint Leslie's work.

Claudia looked at the jumbled heap of books on the floor and gave a shake of her head. She asked Dutch, "You have a char, of course?"

"A what?"

"*Ein Dienstmädchen.*"

It irked him that she resorted to German in such a condescending way instead of explaining the unfamiliar word in English. Stiffly, he replied, "There is no cleaning woman."

"There would appear to be no one here at all, except us," she said.

75

"The men are on the range, rounding up the cattle and branding the calves."

"And the women?"

"There are no women."

"What!" She glared at him indignantly. "You don't expect me to leave this poor child alone here without a woman in attendance!"

"Here, in the West, is sometimes but one woman alone for many miles," he told her. "By my ranch, is better. There is a town not far away. There is a church. By a day's ride are many women for company for her."

Claudia harrumphed as if she found the situation totally unacceptable.

In a small voice, Hannchen said, "Is seem very — uh — loneway."

"Lonesome," Claudia corrected.

Hannchen said, "Always, I have sisters. Always I have live in village. Is very livesome."

"Lively," Claudia said.

Hannchen sighed.

Claudia addressed Dutch again. "I trust you have arranged some form of accommodations for us?"

"There are two rooms." He opened the door of the bedroom that had been Slim Walker's. Claudia took a look inside.

The room was sparsely furnished, just a bed, a dresser, a commode, and a single hide-bottomed chair. All of the personal belongings that had given it character and made it a home to the ranch foreman were at the bunkhouse. The room seemed barren. And wrecked as well.

The drawers had been pulled from the dresser and the commode. The feather bed had been dragged from the bedframe and thrown on the floor. The chair lay on its side. The enameled metal pitcher and basin from the commode were on the floor. A new dent had been added to the many that the pitcher had acquired through long service.

"This!" Claudia sounded aghast.

The room could be put back together easily enough, Dutch thought. He said, "It is good room. Good bed. Better than many."

"It is hardly suitable as a boudoir for a lady," Claudia snapped.

Hannchen said wistfully, "Is very plain."

"You want a picture for the wall?" Dutch asked her.

"Is be nice."

Claudia said, "And curtains for the windows and a carpet for the floor and a reading lamp and suitable chairs."

Wearily, Dutch said, "I will get what is necessary."

"And bedclothes," Claudia went on. "You *do* use bedclothes in this wilderness, don't you, Mr. Falke?"

"There are blankets. Thick clean blankets."

"And sheets?"

Nodding, he grabbed an edge of the feather bed and hauled it back onto its frame. He began shoving the drawers into the dresser. Hannchen watched him a moment, then collected the pitcher and basin. She looked at them with disappointment as she set them on the commode.

Straightening the chair, Dutch said, "There is also another room."

"Better than this?" Claudia asked.

"The same as this."

She sighed as if all were hopeless.

Dutch looked at Hannchen. The disappointment was clear in her eyes. He told her, "In the morning, you can go to town, buy what is needed."

Hannchen turned to Claudia. "Perhaps with curtains . . ."

"Perhaps." Claudia sounded as if she seriously doubted that curtains, or anything else, would help. "Mr. Falke, will you be so kind as to bring in our luggage?"

He ached. He didn't feel like bothering with the cases and trunks. But there was no one else to do it. Without speaking, he went to the surrey and began hauling the luggage into the house. Once that was done, he tended the team and stowed the surrey in the wagon shed. Finally finished with the necessary chores, he went to his own bedroom.

It, too, had been torn apart. The bedding and the drawers from his desk were scattered on the floor. The papers from the drawers and pigeonholes had been stripped out and piled in a heap. The oil lamp sat next to them, its well open as if someone had intended pouring coal oil on the papers and burning them. It looked as if the act might have been interrupted, the culprit frightened away. Frowning, Dutch hunkered and sorted through the papers. He couldn't find the bill of sale for the sorrel filly.

The face of the woman who had fled the kitchen was vivid in his mind. A thin pinched face, more delicate in its line and bone than the faces of those three farmers, but with similar features. Probably she was one of them, most likely their sister.

He stood and stretched, testing the soreness in his body. His shoulder hurt. Stiff and weary, he longed to soak in a hot tub, then stretch out for a good sleep. But there was business to be tended to. Already too much time had been wasted with Hannchen and Claudia.

He changed to riding clothes and strapped on his gun belt. The women were in a bedroom unpacking. He called to them that he would be gone for a while. Claudia acknowledged the information without comment.

Dutch went outside to search the yard.

Hoofs made only slight marks in the hard-pack. He found one print of a big piepan hoof near the edge of the woods behind the house, and fresh droppings that told him the horse had been standing awhile.

Within the woods, he found more marks where hoofs had turned the lush leaf mold. The lumbering plow horses were hardly light-footed. The trail among the trees was clear enough. Collecting a mount for himself, he set out to follow it.

The farmers had kept to the woods. Their trail led back across the slope and skirted a meadow, then turned down-slope toward the Casey River.

In this part of the valley, the woods stopped short of the water, leaving a flood plain along the banks of the river. The grass on the plain was some of the best in the area. Dutch knew this was the grass Quint Leslie envied — and meant to have.

He was still within the woods when he spotted the dirt-dunned Osnaburg top of a wagon beyond the trees. He moved cautiously toward it. The horse he rode was a clever red roan that could stalk a white-tailed buck through the forest with the care of a panther.

Sensitive to the man in the saddle, the roan took Dutch closer to the wagon as noiselessly as if it carried him toward game. Staying to cover within the woods, he found a vantage point overlooking the camp site and drew rein.

The wagon had been pulled up parallel to the river. The two big plow horses were staked nearby and were busy filling their bellies with Dutch's good grass. Between the wagon and the woods, a fire had been built. The haunch of a young calf was spitted over it.

A woman in a baggy dress faded to a dull gray, and a once-white apron soiled to almost the same shade, was bent over the fire ladling sauce from a tin bucket onto the meat. A sunbonnet of calico hid her face.

She seemed too small and withered to be the woman Dutch had seen in his kitchen. He sidled his horse slightly, hoping for a better look at her. The move startled a crow in a tree over his head. It let out a curse. The woman at the fire glanced up. Straight toward Dutch. But she gave no sign she saw him. She returned to basting the meat. When she straightened up, she called in a voice that screeched like a dry wagon wheel, "Pa, you resting easy?"

The wagon rocked slightly. The Osnaburg fluttered. It caught Dutch's attention. He saw the small tears in the side of the wagon top, and a bit of something dark poking through one rip. Someone inside the wagon was aiming the muzzle of a gun through the tear.

A man's voice, old and thin, replied to the woman, "I sure am, Ma. I'm restin' real easy."

They were a sly pair, Dutch thought. They had been expecting trouble and were ready for it. The woman's question had been a signal to the old man inside the wagon that someone was nearby. He wondered if the boys he hunted were hidden in the woods close to the wagon.

Taut, he listened to the small sounds among the trees around him. If the farmers were in the woods, they were managing to be damned quiet.

He considered the possibility that the old man in the wagon might shoot on sight. The day before, when the three young farmers had attacked him, they hadn't meant to kill. They had sounded frightened and surprised when they thought they'd done it. If they had decided to go for his hide, they'd had chance enough to bushwhack him. He doubted that they, or the old people at the wagon, really wanted to commit cold-blooded murder.

Even so, his hand rested on his thigh close to the butt of his revolver as he moved his horse toward the wagon and shouted a hello.

"Why, hello there yourself!" the woman answered, putting on a show of surprise as Dutch rode from the edge of the woods.

Halting, he looked down at her. She was short and stooped at the shoulders. When she tilted her head to look at him, he could see the face under her sunbonnet. It was gaunt and wrinkled. The nose and chin reached toward each other. The thin mouth stretched into a shape resembling a smile of welcome. "Step down and set a spell, mister. I got some vittles cooking here if you'd fancy taking poor fare with poor folk."

Dutch made no move to dismount. He said, "You know this is Falcon range you are camp on?"

She widened her eyes. "It is? Shucks, me and Pa didn't figure it was nothing special. Open land. You know. There ain't no fences around it to tell a body different."

"Cattle range is not to be fenced."

She gave a shake of her head. "Then how's folks to know when they're on it?"

"I am telling you."

"You telling us to get off it?"

Dutch gestured at the wagon. "I would prefer we discuss the matter without a gun at me pointed."

The woman gave a short bark of a laugh, as if she admired Dutch's sharp eye. She called, "Pa, you must've done wagged your tail feathers. Might as well come on out where he can see the rest of you."

The wagon swayed and creaked. The head that poked from under an Osnaburg flap was a match for the woman's. It, too, was old and gaunt-featured. There was a thin rumpled fuzz of white hair on the top, a pair of jug-handle ears, and a tobacco-stained ruff of chin whiskers that didn't completely hide the loose wattles

82

from jaw to neck. The shoulders that followed the head were thin, clad in tattered flannel. A pair of gnarled hands brought out a double-barreled shotgun.

The old man had on breeches that were too big for him. They hung loosely from dull red galluses. His feet were bare. He lowered himself stiffly from the wagon and stood with his legs aspraddle. Dutch thought he looked as if he had been sickly and wasn't quite over it yet. But there was grim determination in the old man's face, and in the way he held the gun.

He gave a hoarse racking cough, spat, then nodded at Dutch sociably and said, "Howdy, stranger. We be the Tatums, Ma and me."

"You know who I am," Dutch said.

The old man cocked a brow at him. "How would we know that?"

"You are expect me."

"Are we?"

"You know I have business with your sons."

"Ain't got no sons," the woman snapped, an acid bitterness in her voice. "Lost two of the boys at Spotsylvania, and one to a bad woman, and the other to a fever. Ain't got no sons left."

She sounded as though she was telling the truth. Dutch eyed the old man, certain he could see a likeness to the three young farmers. He suggested, "Perhaps they are your sons by another wife?"

The old man shook his head. "Had me a boy by my first missus, but she tooken him with her when she run off and I never seen him since."

"There are three young men who be with you." Dutch nodded at the plow horses. "The three who ride those horses."

Tatum eyed him narrowly. "You seen three boys riding our horses?"

"Is waste, so many words." Dutch sighed. "I have business, perhaps, with the men. I have quarrel with them, but is not so important it cannot be settled. Other matters are more important. I have job to be done. I wish to hire men to do it. Perhaps the three who I have seen ride those horses."

"A job?" the woman grunted. She scowled skeptically at Dutch. "For our — for them three boys?"

"Yes."

"You expect us to believe that? You think we'd be dumb enough to flag them boys into a trap for you?" Tatum said.

"Why should I try to trap them? My quarrel with them can be settled to profit for me and for them. Is no need for to fight."

The old woman spoke up. "There's two kinds of words, mister. There's a kind that's as good as gold on any market, and there's the kind that ain't nothing but a lot of wind."

"Believe me if you will," Dutch answered. "Or fight me if you wish. I can fight."

"Can you fight a shotgun?" Tatum's hands were tight on the weapon he held. The muzzle was steady as it pointed at Dutch.

"That would not be wise," Dutch said. "Then you would have the law and also my hired hands to fight. I

84

have large crew. Good men. They are loyal to me. For me, they will kill."

Tatum's eyes darted, scanning the woods. "You ain't got no men with you now."

"No. I have come here to talk, not to fight."

"If you got such a big crew, like you say, what you need with more men?"

"I will talk to them. You will give them my message, yes? Tell them I give my word, if they will come talk and start no trouble, I will start none, yes?"

Lifting rein, Dutch turned his back on the shotgun and rode toward the woods.

CHAPTER
SEVEN

Dutch felt an itching along his spine until he was well within the forest, and well out of the sights of that shotgun. When the itching finally stopped, he reined in and dismounted. The tension had started his sore muscles to aching again. Afoot, he stretched to ease them.

The scent of the woman's cooking lingered in his mind. That sauce she used had a savory tang. He supposed the meat had come from a Falcon calf. Perhaps he should have reclaimed it before he left their camp.

Damn these nesters. He wished to hell they would stay off his land. He hoped those three clodhoppers would come and listen to reason. They had already caused him enough trouble and cost him enough in time and pain and dead animals. He didn't want a fight with them. He wanted to have some good use of them in exchange for what they had cost him.

A sudden sound grabbed his attention. Brush rustled off to his right. Something — or someone — was coming through the underbrush toward him.

His hand went to his revolver. It halted there, wrapped around the gun butt, forefinger on the trigger and thumb on the hammer. He stood with the gun half-drawn. His move was automatic. His mind told him this was no ambush. That wasn't any bushwhacker sneaking through the underbrush intent on his blood. There was no attempt at stealth in the rattle of the bushes. Whatever was coming through the forest was hurrying toward him, making enough noise to spook every wild creature within a hundred yards.

Stepping around the roan's head, he faced the sounds.

It was a woman who came through the woods. He recognized her. She was the same one who had been in his kitchen.

She had her skirts clutched in her left hand, held high, showing her ankles. Her bare feet were dirty. Her ankles were trim and well turned.

Her right hand was tucked under her apron as if she held something hidden there.

Coming within sight of Dutch, she stopped. She was breathing heavily as she called, "Don't try nothing, mister! I got a gun pointing at you here!"

"Have you?" Dutch lifted a brow at her. He was tempted to laugh and call her bluff. But he could see the fear in her, and the effort it was taking her to overcome that fear. With respect for her courage, he slid his hand away from his revolver and held it out, the empty palm toward her.

The fine edge of her fear softened slightly. She came a step closer to him. Within the shadows of the woods, he couldn't make out the color of her eyes. He remembered that they were brown. A vivid warm brown.

Her face was too thin, too sharp in the bone, yet not unattractive with its pert nose and wide full mouth. Her dress and apron were like old woman Tatum's, faded with much lye-soap scrubbing and grayed with ground-in dirt. The apron had been patched several times. The dress was too big, hanging from her shoulders. The soft cloth only hinted at the small firm breasts and gently rounded hips it hid.

As he looked her over, he thought that with a bath, some decent clothes, and a few good meals to fill out her frame, she would be rather a pretty woman.

"I don't mean you no harm, mister," she said, trying to sound as if she were capable of doing him great harm, should she wish to.

He said, "What do you want of me?"

"You leave my brothers alone! You got no call to go hang them! They didn't mean to kill you, you hear?"

"You think I am intend to hang them?"

She cocked her head, looking surprised at his calm, quiet tone and the denial implicit in his words. "Don't you?"

"It is not my custom to hang men."

"But they say — we heard — folks say you hanged . . ." Her voice faded. With a kind of animal wariness, she asked, "What *do* you mean to do to them?"

"Hire them, if they will work for me and do the job I am pay them for."

"*Hire them?*"

"I am need some men. I think perhaps your brothers need money."

"You don't mean to kill them?"

"Why should I kill them?"

"After what they done to you — we heard — you're supposed to be — I thought —" She stopped, unable to express what she meant.

He almost smiled at her. There was something quite charming about her. She put him in mind of the gentle wild creatures of the forest and range, the soft-eyed fawns and mustang fillies. He told her, "They did foolish things. It was very foolish to enter my house and do much damage and steal the bill of sale for the horse. Did they think to steal the paper would end the problem?"

"Sometimes they ain't too smart," she admitted. "Mostly when they been drinking."

"If they come to work for me, then they must not drink." He eyed her with curiosity, remembering that careful heap of broken glass next to the lamp table. "You were in my house, too. But not to damage and destroy, I think."

She gave a bit of a nod. "I followed them. I was afraid — I didn't know what they meant to do. Soon as I got there, I scared them off, but they'd already made an awful mess of things. I'm sorry about that, mister. I meant to get it all cleaned up the best I could, only you come back too soon. I'm sorry —"

"Why did you run away?"

"What would you 've done if you was me and you'd 've come on me like that with a gun in your hand?"

He cocked a brow at her. "As you have a gun in your hand now?"

She blinked and darted a look at her apron where one hand was hidden.

"It is poor bluff," he told her. "Dangerous bluff."

"Huh?"

"It is not wise to threaten armed man with a gun you do not have."

Her eyes narrowed. "What makes you think I don't have a gun?"

"If you have one, you would be show it."

She hesitated, trying to think of an answer to that. She couldn't. Angrily, she said, "You knew all along! You just been funning me!"

He shook his head. "I have been listen to you. I hope you have listen to me. I do not want to shoot anyone. I do not want trouble. I want to keep what is mine. I want payment for what has from me been taken. Your brothers have kill one of my wild horses and have steal a valuable filly from me. They have beat me and make accusations against me in public, and make wreck in my house. They have steal the paper of the filly from me. In your camp, their horses my grass eat. I think your brothers my beef eat. This makes to me a great debt they owe. I think revenge is not enough payment. I do not profit by revenge."

"We don't have no money! We can't hardly pay you for no mess of stuff like that!" she protested.

"I will accept payment by work. Good work, with they be loyal to me."

"*I'll* work for you," she said. "I'll come fix up the mess they made out of your house. I'll come do it right now. Will that help, mister?"

"Perhaps," he said thoughtfully. Claudia Prescott had wanted a cleaning woman at the ranch. It might be a help to Hannchen to have another woman around. "Can you keep house, do washing, cook?"

She nodded.

"Do you want to come live by my house, work for me?"

Wariness crept into her voice. "*Live* at your house?"

"Yes."

"Alone? With you?"

"Not alone. There are women at my house. Two women."

"What kind of women?" she asked suspiciously.

"Very respectable women," he assured her. "A young woman from Hesse who is soon to be my wife, and an Englishwoman who is by her the teacher and chaperone."

"If you got two women there now, what you need me there for?" She didn't sound reassured.

He smiled at her. "My new bride is strange to this country. She is young and is need help, need to learn. She is need another woman for company when the Englishwoman is gone. The Englishwoman is not good for to do chores in a house, I think. She is very — ah — sour."

"You don't like her?"

"It is my wish to marry quickly so she will be gone. Will you come and be help and friend to my Hannchen?"

"What's a Hannchen?"

"It is a name. The name of the woman I will be marry. What name is to call you?"

"Rosy. My name is Rosy Tatum."

"Will you come work by me, Rosy Tatum?"

She studied him a long, thoughtful moment. Lowering her eyes, she said, "I expect maybe — I think — uh huh, if it's all right with Ma and Pa."

"The old ones at the wagon are to you Ma and Pa?" He remembered the old woman claiming that the boys were not her sons. He had thought there was a ring of truth to her words.

"Rightly, they're Grandma and Grandpa," Rosy told him. "Only we lost our real Ma and Pa a long time back and our grandfolks been raising us all since we was pups, and we got to calling them Ma and Pa. It's just like they really was."

It pleased Dutch to learn that the old woman hadn't been lying after all — even if she had been twisting the truth to her own purposes.

Catching a stirrup, he started up to the saddle. "Come. I will take you back by them. You can talk about working for me."

She dropped the stick she had been hiding under her apron, pretending it was a gun, and came up to his side. He held out a hand to help her onto the horse. She reached for it, then suddenly pulled back.

Sniffing the air, she looked over her shoulder toward the camp. It was well behind her, beyond a stretch of woods. She couldn't see it. But she frowned as if something about it had disturbed her.

92

Dutch caught the scent of smoke. It smelled as if something damp had been flung on a fire. Something like the wet blankets the Indians used to produce signal puffs of smoke.

Drawing back, Rosy said, "No, you wait here. I'll go talk to them. You wait right here! You promise! I'll be back quick!"

Gathering her skirts, she scurried off.

Dutch called after her, "Tell the brothers what I have told you. Bring them back with you and I talk to them here, now."

She halted sharply and looked at him.

"I know the old ones have signaled for them to return to the wagon," he said. "I think you will be see them there. From me, give them the message, yes?"

She didn't reply, but gazed at him a moment, then disappeared into the woods.

Stepping down from the horse again, he looped the reins on a bush. Then he drew his revolver and checked it. He slipped it back into the holster and felt the set of it. Loose and easy. It would come quickly to hand, if need be. Flexing his fingers, he walked away from the horse.

In the brush, he hunkered to wait. He was certain that he had convinced Rosy Tatum of his sincerity. Certain she believed he did not mean to harm her brothers. He was not so certain she could convince them of that.

It took a long time. Finally he heard faint sounds in the woods. Soft, stealthy footsteps. Intent, he concentrated on their location.

He decided that two of the brothers were moving out to the sides, meaning to flank him. Drawing his gun, he stretched out on his belly and squirmed into a thicket of underbrush.

The brothers stopped moving. There was silence. Then a call.

"Hallo! Mr. Falke?"

The voice belonged to the oldest brother, Wade.

Dutch remained silent.

"Falke?" Wade called. "I've come to talk, like you wanted."

Still Dutch made no reply.

"Show yourself!" Wade shouted.

Dutch waited.

From his left, he heard the brother Rob sing out, "He's got to be around here somewheres! I got a bead on his horse!"

"Likely he's got a bead on you!" Wade answered, sounding disgusted at his brother.

Rob asked, "What do I do now?"

"Get the hell gone before he shoots you!" Wade's voice was anxious, as if he were about to break and run himself.

"No!" That was Rosy's voice. It came from the same direction as Wade's. "I told you, he don't mean you no trouble! He only wants to talk to you!"

"Then why don't he show himself?" Wade demanded.

Dutch heard footfalls to his left. It sounded as if Rob was going to join Wade and the girl. He listened for some sound from the man on the right. There was none. Stony was still in position.

Rob reached his brother and Rosy. He spoke softly, but his voice carried in the stillness of the forest. "What do you think, Wade?"

"I think he's hid around here somewhere waiting to pick us off, first chance he gets."

"No!" Rosy insisted.

"Shut up before he gets his sights on you," Wade told her.

"Oh, you!" she snapped. Dutch heard a rustle of brush. Then Rosy was running toward his horse, calling, "Mr. Falke! Don't shoot, Mr. Falke! It's me! I brung my brothers to talk to you like you said!"

She halted beside the horse and turned around, scanning the trees. "Mr. Falke? Where are you, Mr. Falke?"

"Rosy, you get down!" Wade shouted at her. He came bulling through the brush, grabbing for her to pull her back to cover. He had his rifle in one hand. He snatched for Rosy's wrist with the other.

As Rosy ran to the horse, Dutch braced himself to move. Revolver at the ready, he flung himself up onto his feet and lunged toward Wade.

The sight of Dutch, and the gun, startled Wade. For an instant, he froze. Then he was letting go Rosy's wrist, trying to swing up the rifle.

Dutch slammed his empty hand at the rifle barrel, knocking it aside, and punched the muzzle of the revolver into Wade's gut.

Wade jerked back.

"Stop!" Dutch snapped at him.

Rosy gasped. She pressed a hand to her mouth, then brought it away and swung it at Dutch's face. It hit, palm open. A sharp, stinging slap.

"Stop!" Dutch snarled at her. "All stop, or I shoot the brother!"

Rosy drew back, her eyes wide with fear and anger and disappointment.

Wade dropped the rifle and lifted his hands.

"Call the others," Dutch told him.

Wade gave a slow shake of his head. "So's you can shoot us all down? No sir!"

"I will shoot no one, unless it is forced," Dutch told him. "I wish to talk. Your sister has told you I wish to talk. You will not talk. You are come here like wolves to surround me. Come now to face me like men. Understand?"

"If you only want to talk, what the hell you got that gun in my gut for?"

"Why are you have guns pointing for me while I am wait for you?"

Rosy spoke up. "They didn't trust you."

"So?" Dutch said. "Why now should I trust them?"

Wade was handling himself well, but the revolver Dutch held nuzzled against his belly was wearing on his nerves. His face shone with sweat. His voice was jerky as he said, "Dammit, whatever this is all about, let's get it the hell over with!"

"Then call out from hiding the others so we can talk," Dutch told him.

Wade took a breath and let it out with a sigh. Then he shouted, "Stony! Rob! You come out to where he can see you. Only don't you let your sights off him, you hear?"

The two brothers emerged slowly from the brush. Rob had a rifle. Stony carried a shotgun. Both looked scared.

Dutch recognized the weapons as the ones missing from his own gun rack. He said, "Put down the guns."

Wade shook his head.

Rosy suggested to Dutch, "You put your gun down."

Dutch smiled at her and gestured for her to come closer. She lifted her brows in question. He held his free hand out to her. "Here. Come by me. Trust me. Or to this quarrel there may be no ending."

He could see that she wanted to trust him. She sidled cautiously toward him. Her fingers closed on his and he could feel the trembling in them. He tugged, pulling her up to his side.

Then he dropped his revolver into its holster. As he did it, he held Wade's eyes with his, and spoke to the others. "Put down the guns."

Stony acted first. It was obvious that he couldn't trigger the shotgun at Dutch without the pellets spreading to take his sister as well. Gently, he set the shotgun on the ground.

When Rob saw his brother give in, he put down the rifle.

Dutch felt the sudden relief in his gut like a spring unwinding. He darted Rosy a grin. She smiled back at him and her hand gave his a quick press.

Wade still had his arms in the air. He frowned at Dutch. "You mean it? You really want to *talk* to us?"

97

"Yes," Dutch said.

"Yes!" Rosy echoed, sounding proud that her faith in Dutch had been justified.

Wade moved one hand to wipe at the sweat on his forehead. He discovered the other hand was still in the air and lowered it. Glancing at his brothers, he said, "All right, Stony, Rob, come on over here. I reckon we all got some talking to do."

CHAPTER
EIGHT

Wade was wary, but he was willing to try making peace with Dutch. He said, "We didn't want what happened out there yesterday. I mean, when we thought we'd killed you. We sure as hell didn't want to do that."

Stony looked sheepish and belligerent at the same time, as if the near-killing had embarrassed him. He grumbled, "*You* started it."

Cocking a brow at him, Dutch answered, "You had no business to shoot the wild stallion."

"It was about to kill Stony!" Wade protested.

Dutch shook his head. "I had on it my rope. I had it stopped. You shot it."

"*I* didn't figure you had it stopped. I couldn't take no chance. Not on Stony getting killed," Wade said. He sounded sincere. And fiercely loyal to his brothers.

Stony nodded in agreement.

Dutch could see their point of view. They weren't rangewise. They hadn't known his skill with a rope, or realized he had the stallion under control.

Wanting to know them better and see the workings of their minds, he kept up the argument. "You have no business trying the stallion to steal."

"We sure as hell didn't know it belonged to nobody," Wade told him. "We heard anything on the range without a brand didn't belong to nobody and was free for the taking."

"So you steal the filly I was ride because she wore no brand. You think she was free for the taking?"

"We thought you was dead," Rob put in. "It wouldn't 've mattered about us taking her if you was dead, would it?"

Stony spoke up, sounding almost anguished. "Mister, you don't know how bad I need a horse! I didn't mean to steal one, but I sure as hell need one! We ain't got but those two old plow plugs between the three of us. It ain't no good, two men on one horse!"

"We all need horses," Wade said. "We just got them two nags to pull the wagon. With all of us on board, it's a hard pull for them. We been letting Ma and Pa ride and the rest of us been walking most of the way since we crossed the Missouri. Now we got to get us work of some kind and we need some way we can get around, and we can't hardly do it on just them two old nags."

"You understand, don't you, Mr. Falke?" Rosy said. "We can't just keep moving on. We got mountains ahead of us to climb. Pa's took poorly and we ain't got no money left. We got to make us a stake and get some stock and supplies before we set out over the mountains. We got to get some money."

Dutch eyed Wade askance. "You are have money enough to go by the Red Rooster to drink."

"We shouldn't 've done that," Wade admitted. "We'd sold a calf and had a couple of dollars and we should 've put it to better use. Only, after we thought we'd killed you, we started on the jug at the wagon, and after we'd done some drinking it seemed like it'd be real fine to do some more in a nice place like that Red Rooster. That was the likker doing our thinking for us. It wasn't the right thing to do at all."

"You sold a calf?" Dutch growled at him.

"It didn't have no brand on it!" Stony said. "It didn't belong to nobody!"

Rob added, "They got a name for them calves like that. I heard all about it. A calf without no brand, it's called — called —" He couldn't remember.

Stony remembered. "A maverick! Them kind belong to anybody can catch them." He turned to Wade. "That's so, ain't it?"

Nodding, Wade said to Dutch, "That there wasn't nobody's calf, mister. We were sure of that 'fore we took it."

"Was it weaned or suckling?" Dutch asked.

Wade shrugged.

"A calf is be a maverick only after it is weaned and is from its mother apart," Dutch told them. "It is a maverick if there is no way to know the brand on the mother cow. On *my* range, all calves are mine."

"We sure as hell didn't know that!" Wade said.

Dutch answered, "You know now."

"We sure done messed up a lot since we been here," Stony mumbled.

Wade said to Dutch, "We won't take no more of your calves."

"You have enough taken already. How many? Six? Eight?"

"Only three!" Rosy protested. "That's all! One we et up already and the one we're cutting off and the one we sold! That's all! I swear it, Mr. Falke!"

"Three is enough. You will pay me for them?"

"How?" Wade asked. "We told you, we ain't got no money."

"Rosy said you had work for us?" Stony said hopefully.

Rob agreed, "Rosy and the folks all told us you said you might hire us on, Mr. Falke."

Wade eyed Dutch. "Was that just a flag to pull us out here where you could get your sights on us, or you really mean it?"

"I mean it," Dutch replied. "There is rancher by the other side of the river. Quint Leslie —"

"I heard of him," Stony interrupted. "I heard his outfit is bigger'n yourn."

Dutch nodded. "He is intend to drive cattle across the river onto my range. I need men to ride the river and warn me when Quint tries to move his cattle across."

"And fight him for you?" Wade asked.

"Perhaps."

"You mean for us to go up against this Quint Leslie and maybe get killed just to keep him off your land?" Rob said.

"Perhaps. But I have on the range a crew, and when it is time, I will call them to join in the fight. But I do not wish to stop roundup to have them make patrol. I will hire you to ride patrol and give warning so I can call in the crew. Yes?"

Stony grumbled, "We can't hardly ride no patrols on them old plow horses of ours."

"If you come to work by me, I will provide horses to use," Dutch told him.

Stony's eyes widened with eager interest. He looked as if he wanted a decent mount more than anything else in life.

"And I will provide the use of the guns you have already *borrowed* from me." Dutch glanced significantly at the weapons on the ground.

"We ain't really thieves," Wade said. "Only we was in so deep by then, it didn't seem no worse to profit by it."

The other brothers nodded. Rosy glared at them as if she hadn't known about the theft of the guns. "That ain't no excuse to go stealing!"

"It was foolish to wreck the house and take the bill of sale for the filly," Dutch said.

"Yeah, I reckon," Wade agreed with a sigh. He hesitated, torn between his pride and embarrassment. "Only — Mr. Falke, I'll tell you the truth of it. We was scared. We figured if you gave that paper to the marshal in town, it might go hard with us. We thought — we was kind of hoping we could spook you off. Show you we could make trouble for you, even if we are only poor folk."

"We been pushed around a lot," Rob said. "Comes a time a man takes a notion to push back."

Stony nodded. "There was fellers in town told us you was — uh — kind of mean. They said you'd hang us all if you got the chance."

"They told you I have hang men before?" Dutch asked.

Stony gave another nod.

Dutch knew the rumors. He didn't bother to ask more. Spreading his fingers, he began to count. "You are owe me for dead stallion, for three calves, for damage to my house, and for the anger you have cause me. You owe me at least one month work, each of you."

The brothers and Rosy exchanged unhappy glances.

Wade spoke for them. "That might be so, Mr. Falke, only we can't do it. Somebody's got to take care of our folks. Somebody's got to keep them in vittles. We got to make us a stake to move on with. We can't all work for you for a whole month without no pay."

The protest pleased Dutch. If the Tatums had agreed readily to his proposal, he would have suspected they were lying and meant to run out on him.

He told them, "I will provide by you horses and guns and ammunition. I will pay to each of you five dollars now in cash. When the month is done, if I have more need of you, I will pay five dollars for each man for each week. Yes?"

He gestured at Rosy. "If your sister is come to work by my house, I give her keep, and if she is stay when the month is done, I pay her three dollars a week."

"Three dollars!" Rosy gasped.

Wade eyed Dutch. "You could get some girl out an orphanage to do the work for just her keep and nothing more."

"Yes." Dutch felt a little rash making such a generous offer, but he liked Rosy Tatum. He wanted to help her.

Suspiciously, Wade said, "Just what is it you want my sister to do for this here three dollars a week?"

"Keep house and be companion to my wife."

"You got a wife?"

Dutch explained briefly about the girl he was to wed. He added, "If my Hannchen is liking your sister, then Rosy is be worth the money. If Hannchen is not liking her, or she is not doing good work, then perhaps I get from an orphanage a girl."

"Oh, I'll do the work fine!" Rosy exclaimed. "I promise! Wait till you taste my vittles! I can cook real good, Mr. Falke! And mend and darn and wash! I can make the sweetest soft soap you ever touched a hand to!"

"And be the friend to my Hannchen?"

"I'll try! I'll try awful hard!"

"That's all you want from Rosy?" Wade asked.

Dutch nodded.

"And what you want from us is to ride along the river and keep watch for cattle starting across?"

"By day and by night."

Wade questioned his brothers with his eyes. Their faces answered him. He told Dutch, "It's agreed, Mr. Falke."

"I expect loyalty."

"You got our word."

"Is good. Now you are get horses from the remuda at roundup camp." Dutch tugged a tally book from his pocket. He wrote a short note, ripped the page from the book, and handed it to Wade. "You take this to my foreman. It tells him to provide to you the horses. When you have them, come by my house."

Wade folded the note and tucked it into his hatband. "Yes, sir."

Hunkering, Dutch brushed away a patch of dead leaves to bare the earth under them. He sketched a map as he told the Tatums how to locate the roundup camp. When he was sure they understood, he wiped out the map with his boot sole, then kicked the leaves back.

As he collected his mount, he asked Rosy, "You come in the morning with the brothers?"

Her face was solemn, but her eyes shone as she replied, "I can come now, if you want."

He stepped up onto the horse. Holding a hand out to her, he said, "Then come."

She took the hand, put a bare foot on the toe of his stirruped boot, and swung up behind him on the horse. He gigged the roan into a fast walk. Rosy waved and called a goodbye to her brothers.

They had cleared the woods and were on a trail back to the ranch house when she spoke. "What's wrong with your arm, Mr. Falke?"

"Is nothing wrong."

"The way you use it, looks like maybe you're hurting."

"Is nothing. A sprain perhaps."

"In the shoulder?"

106

"Yes."

"I can help. When you get to home, I can make up a plaster that'll draw the soreness. Might be a good rub would help now." She put her palms to the back of his shoulder and began to knead at the aching muscles.

At first it hurt so much that he almost winced. But as she worked at it, the soreness began to ease. Her touch was firm but not rough. It was very pleasant. He smiled slightly to himself, thinking it would be good to have a woman rub away the stiffness in such a manner when he had come in from a day's hard riding. Would Hannchen have such a skill in her hands, he wondered.

As they raised the ranch house, he was surprised to see a saddle horse at the hitch rail. He recognized it as one of the hacks Tinker Jim kept for hire. So he had a caller. One who didn't keep a horse of his own.

Drawing rein next to the hack, he swung a leg over the saddle bow. He dropped to the ground and offered Rosy his hands. She slid into them. For an instant he held her, his hands on her upper arms. She was very close. Her face was turned up toward his. Her flesh was warm under his fingers. Her mouth seemed very inviting. Her eyes, meeting his, were a dark velvety brown, filled with warmth.

It would not be right to kiss her, he told himself. Not while his bride-to-be was waiting in the house for him. And not when he had given Rosy his word that he would respect her honor.

He dropped his hands from her arms. She turned from him, starting toward the house. He stood a moment, watching her from the back. As she walked, there was a soft flowing grace to her whole body. He felt as if he could contentedly stand there and watch her walk for the rest of the day.

He gave a shake of his head to rid himself of such thoughts. Long-striding, he caught up with her and jerked open the door for her. The courtesy brought a smile to her lips and put a fresh touch of pride into her bearing as she stepped inside.

Dutch followed her in. The living room was no longer the shambles he had left. The chairs and tables were upright again, the rugs straight, and the books and curios back on the shelves. The chairs had been moved around. The four that had been in a loose semicircle facing the fireplace were now grouped together facing each other. The low chest that had been up against a wall was in the center of the circle made by the chairs. A table scarf had been draped over it. A biscuit sheet rested on the scarf, serving as a tray for the coffeepot and sugar tin.

Hannchen, Claudia, and James Easton sat in the chairs, each holding a cup. As Dutch and Rosy entered, Easton stood. He gave Rosy a slight bow, then offered Dutch a nod of greeting. Claudia wrinkled her forehead in a look of both query and disapproval as she peered at Rosy. Hannchen glanced uncertainly from Rosy to Dutch and back again.

Dutch glared at Easton. "What are you do here?"

"Mr. Falke!" Claudia exclaimed. Her voice was sternly reprimanding. "Mr. Easton has been kind enough to call on us and to help us restore order to this room! He is a *guest* in this house!"

The house belonged to Dutch, not to the Englishwoman. It was his right to say who might and might not be a guest in it. He disliked Easton. He disliked the fact that Easton's company pleased the women so much more than his own did. He answered darkly, "An uninvited guest!"

"By no means!" Claudia snapped back at him. "Mr. Easton is an *invited* guest! He is here at *my* invitation!"

"If my presence offends Mr. Falke, ladies, I am afraid I must take leave of you," Easton said to Claudia and Hannchen. His voice was cool and as slick as suet.

"*Ach nein!*" Hannchen looked distressed. She turned to Dutch. "*Sie* — Herr — Mr. Falke, it is — Mr. Easton is not mean to offend. He is nice. Good to us by travel. He is help us much."

"He has been very kind to us," Claudia said to Dutch. "He is a *gentleman*. I find your unwarranted rudeness to him most appalling."

Dutch didn't give a damn what she thought. His distrust of Easton had been immediate, as instinctive as a stallion's reaction to the scent of a wolf.

Easton set his coffee cup on the makeshift tray. "Please excuse me, ladies. I really must be going."

Claudia scowled at Dutch, then smiled at Easton. Very properly, quite sweetly, she said, "I do hope you'll call again."

Hannchen smiled at Easton, too, as she nodded in agreement with Claudia. Easton answered with a slight bow to each of them, and another to Rosy. He looked at Dutch, his face blank and hard.

Dutch met his eyes coldly, and said nothing.

109

Easton put on his hat and walked out. As he closed the door behind him, Claudia turned angrily on Dutch. "I have never seen such rudeness in my whole life!"

Hannchen gazed at the door a moment. Then, eying Rosy, she spoke to Claudia. *"Wer ist sie?"*

Dutch felt she had spoken in German deliberately so that Rosy wouldn't understand her question. He snapped at her, "I have told you to speak English!"

Hannchen's lip thrust out in a pout.

Rosy was standing close beside Dutch, her nearness asking his protection. The pride of her bearing was stiffly self-conscious. He could sense her discomfort at the scene she had witnessed, and at the sour scrutiny of the women. She was very aware of being a stranger here. He understood that feeling. He had known it often when he first arrived in this country. He still felt it occasionally when he was among those townsfolk who spoke with respect to his face and spread ugly rumors behind his back.

He turned from Hannchen and Claudia as if dismissing them from his consideration. Gently he said to Rosy, "Come. I will show to you the kitchen."

Rosy followed him. He closed the door behind them, shutting out Hannchen and Claudia. Softly he said, "You see? The sooner the marriage is take place, the sooner the old buzzard will go away."

Some of the tension eased away from Rosy. She almost smiled. But her eyes remained solemn as she asked, "You really gonna marry that little girl in there?"

He nodded. "You do not like her?"

110

"I don't know. I ain't hardly met her yet. Who's the stiffcollar you booted out?"

"A *gentleman* they have met on the coach. His name is Easton."

"You sure ain't got much use for him."

"No."

"You think he's got a fancy for your lady friend there?"

Dutch felt sure of it. He didn't like the idea one damned bit. He didn't answer Rosy.

She didn't seem to expect an answer. She had turned away from him to busy herself examining the kitchen. Her brothers had not pulled it apart the way they had the other rooms. Pots and pans were in good order, hanging from nails in the wall. Crockery was in place on the shelves. Foodstuffs were in the pantry. She opened the pantry door and peeked in.

"Gee, you got a mess of good vittles here!" she said. "I never seen so many airtights outside a store. You know, Mr. Falke, any woman who'd take off after the likes of that Mr. Easton might not be worth chasing to fetch her back."

Dutch smiled to himself. Rosy had a directness about her that pleased him. He thought she might be right. But he had an obligation to Herr Onkel Heinrich. He had to take care of Hannchen.

Rosy came out of the pantry carrying a tin can as if it were a very special treasure she had found. "Peaches! You like peaches, Mr. Falke?"

"Yes."

"You reckon it'd be all right if I fixed up a peach cobbler for supper? I ain't had no kind of peach pie for an awful long time."

"That would be fine," he told her. "And perhaps you could find something to be fix now, too? I am hungry."

"Oh!" She looked taken aback, as if she felt she should have realized as much without being told. "Yes! I'll get something going quick!"

"Then the kitchen is yours. If you cannot find what is wanted, call me." He reached for the doorknob. Darting Rosy a quick rueful grin, he added, "I think I must be face the old buzzard again."

She returned his grin. Her eyes sparkled as if she were delighted to share his opinion of Claudia Prescott.

When he went back into the living room, Claudia and Hannchen were still sitting as he had left them. Claudia held a cup in her hand. She glared at Dutch over it.

"Mr. Falke, your house is ill equipped. I could find no decent utensils! No teapot or service or cozy! I couldn't even find the tea! Or the cream! Or any form of cakes! I had to offer our guest the meager substitute of coffee. Served from *tin* cups! It is disgraceful! This whole —" She paused as if she couldn't find a suitable word. With a sweep of the hand that held the cup, she indicated the house, the land around it, perhaps the entire nation. And Dutch in particular. "This whole affair is most disappointing! *Most!*"

"Then it is well that you have no intention of staying longer than is necessary." He picked up the cup Easton had left, sloshed the dregs of coffee in it, then stepped to the door and emptied the coffee on the ground outside. Returning, he filled the cup from the pot and sampled the coffee. He gave a sad shake of his head. "*This* is very much disappointing. It surprises me your guest was willing to drink it."

"I could find no tea!" Claudia answered indignantly.

Hannchen was watching Dutch from under her lashes. She cleared her throat and said, "Who is the woman you are bring by the house?"

"Yes!" Claudia said, her expression implying Dutch was obviously up to no good. "Some *friend* of yours, Mr. Falke?"

"Her name is Rosy Tatum," he told her. "You have suggest there should be a hired girl to help take care of house, so I have bring one."

"That poor creature!" Claudia bobbed her head toward the kitchen where Rosy was busy at work. "Why, she hardly appears civilized! Do you expect *her* to be adequate as a household servant?"

Nothing in this world would please the English-woman, Dutch thought darkly. Certainly nothing he did would please her. He answered, "If Rosy is not satisfy you, I could get from the reservation a squaw to be the maid."

"*Ach, nein!*" Hannchen squeaked.

Claudia gasped, "A savage!"

"Squaws work good," he said. "They take pride. They work hard. They make good wives."

Hannchen squeaked again.

Claudia rose to face Dutch eye to eye. "Mr. Falke, since the moment we arrived, you have extended

113

yourself to make us feel *un*welcome. Your rudeness is unsurpassed. I begin to wonder at the wisdom of leaving this poor child at your mercy!"

"Then take her home to Hesse." He turned to Hannchen. "Do you want to go home to Hesse?"

Before the girl could reply, Claudia was saying, "You intend to reject her? To send her back to her family in disgrace?"

"I think you reject me," he said. "What is your purpose in this, woman? What business is this of yours? It is for you to bring Miss Gerber here safely, and attend her until she is married. Is it your business, too, to make the choice of husband for her?"

Claudia's face paled with anger. The lines of bitterness around her mouth and eyes deepened. "I — I — never — I — !"

She found no words to express herself. Wheeling, she strode to the bedroom and slammed the door behind her.

Hannchen whimpered. Dutch saw dampness forming on her lashes. A tear trembled on one, then rolled down her cheek.

Dammit, he hadn't meant to hurt or frighten her. But the chaperone was like a burr under his saddle, galling him raw. He stood looking sympathetically at Hannchen, wondering what he could say to make her understand.

"It is for you I have brought Rosy Tatum to work here," he told her. "I think it would be help to you. I think you would be glad to have a woman here to be company for you."

"For me, you brought her?" She looked up at him with surprise.

"Yes."

"I was afraid perhaps you — she — I think for *you*, you have brought her. Mr. Falke, do you like me?"

"Of course."

"It is all very strange by me."

"You will learn."

She gave a hopeful little nod.

"Are you so disappointed by me as the English-woman is?" he asked her.

"No," she replied. But it seemed to him that there was a great deal of uncertainty and fear in her eyes.

"Tomorrow, you will go into town and get for your room the curtains and things you are need," he said. "Will that please you?"

"*Ja!* Yes! Is good!" Her outburst of enthusiasm was so powerful that it startled him.

Gazing at her, he gave a puzzled shake of his head. He wondered if he would ever understand her.

CHAPTER
NINE

Eating supper while Claudia Prescott was at the table wasn't pleasant. She found fault with the way the food was prepared, the manner in which Rosy served it, and the fact that Rosy sat at the table to eat with the others instead of standing by to fetch and carry. Finally, in disgust, Dutch told her that the food suited his tastes, and the house was his and would be run as he chose.

Indignantly, Claudia left the table to retire to the bedroom. The ghost of her presence remained. The others finished eating in awkward silence.

When they were done, Dutch told Hannchen to help Rosy with the cleaning up. While the women worked, he settled himself in his favorite chair with a book. For a while he tried to read, but the book failed to hold his attention. His shoulder still ached. He kept thinking of Rosy's strong hands massaging away the soreness. Eventually he put down the book and drifted outside.

The spring nights were cool. The sky was clear and deep, filled with stars. Small breezes played through the woods and over the grass, bringing him scents of fresh green. There was a quiet calm to the night that soothed away harsh tensions.

He thought it might help if he talked to Hannchen in such surroundings, without Claudia nearby. Drifting back to the house, he waited near the kitchen door. Soon one of the women came out to empty the dishpan. It was Rosy.

He called to her, telling her to send Hannchen to him.

She glanced around at the night, the stars, the shadows, then returned to the kitchen slowly, as if she were reluctant to deliver his message.

When Hannchen came from the house, she was walking with her shoulders slumped and her head down.

"Is something wrong?" Dutch asked her.

She lifted her face. Her eyes caught sparks of starlight. Her mouth shaped a small, tremulous pout. "I am not be liking that woman!"

"Rosy?" he asked with surprise.

She nodded.

"Why not?"

"She is make to me as if I am the child still! Everything she tells me, as if I am not know anything at all!"

"She is only trying to help," he suggested.

She shook her head. "She is not liking me. She is want to make me unhappy here. I am telling! Is she have to stay here?"

"Can you run the house alone without someone to help? Can you do all of the cooking and the cleaning and washing and mending by yourself?"

"Is no one else can be housemaid?"

"Cannot you do the work?"

Snuffling, she gave a small shake of her head. "In Hesse, Herr Reiter is tell me you are very rich man. He say to me in America you have fine house with much servants to make do the work!"

Where had Herr Onkel Heinrich gotten such ideas as that, Dutch thought. No wonder Hannchen had been disappointed. She had been expecting a palace, not a working frontier ranch.

He said gently, "Herr Reiter is wrong. You see what my home is. There is much work. I have hire Rosy Tatum to be help to you. She is be much help to you when the Prescott woman is gone."

"Is Frau Prescott must go?"

"As soon as we are married."

"*Nein! Bitte!* I am not want her to be gone!"

"You like her but you do not like Rosy Tatum?" he said, puzzled.

"Frau Prescott is learn me nice things. How to be the proper lady for to live in fine house." She held out her hands, peering at them in the dim starlight. "The proper lady is have the pretty fingers. She is not get them all wrinkled and ugly with the dishwater."

"Or with washing dirty clothes?"

"Yes. The proper lady is have many servants. A cook by the kitchen, a washerwoman and a housemaid and a nice servant girl to say 'Yes, ma'am' and 'No, ma'am' and put on her the dresses and make curtsy so." She demonstrated. Gesturing at the kitchen, she added, "Not like that one."

"Is it so in Hesse?" he asked. "With your mama and papa, are you such a proper lady that you do not wash the dishes yourself, and you have the servants to wait on you?"

"No," she admitted. "But in America is different! Herr Reiter is promise me in America you are the very rich man, like a baron, and you are have the fine house and many men to work for you and many horses. He is promise in America I will be the fine lady by you. He is hire Frau Prescott to teach me right the way I am to be proper lady for your fine house. But this is not — is not — !" She began to cry.

He slipped an arm around her shoulder, pulling her close. She pressed her face against his chest. Holding her, he wondered what he could say to her. He cast back in memory over Herr Onkel's letters about her.

Herr Onkel had bragged that she was no peasant girl but the daughter of a *Bürgermeister*, a girl with schooling, who could read and write. That had seemed an outstanding accomplishment to Herr Onkel. And to Dutch, at the time.

Now he thought perhaps she had read too much. She had filled her head with romantic fantasies and did not know what to expect of real life. She thought America should be like the fairy stories of beautiful princesses and handsome princes living happily ever after in marble castles and ivory towers.

He said to her, "You know that Herr Reiter is to me like the father. From the time my own father and mother died, he is been my family. He is always dream of coming to America, but he is not able to do it

119

himself, so he is raise me to come here and make for myself a good life in this land. Understand?"

He felt her small nod against his chest.

"It is sixteen years since he put me on the boat to come here. I am then younger than you are now. I am then full of the dreams from Herr Onkel Heinrich. He is tell me that the streets in America are not really paved with gold the way some people are saying. But in his heart, I think, he is always believe they are. He is always believe very fine things of America. In much he is right. It is a good country. But it is not so easy here as he is think."

She made a small sound of agreement, as if she had already found her own brief stay almost unbearably difficult.

He went on, "I am not long here when my money is stolen from me. I have nothing. From luck, I find work. Hard work. Like the ox, I work from the dark before sunrise until long after the sun is set. In those days in America, I am cold and hungry and aching sick with weariness. It is take me much work to come here to this place, these mountains, and build this house. Now there is money. There is food and warm clothing and fuel for fires. Now there is much that is good. But there is not endless riches. There is still work. Always there is work. Always there is the new problem to be solved and the new trouble to be faced. There is no end to that but death. Understand?"

She gave another little nod against his chest. He knew she understood his words. He wasn't sure she comprehended his meaning.

120

He told her, "There is no elf gold. There is no magic castle. I am no great prince and you are no enchanted princess. There is no such world as in the stories where all live forever happily. Do you understand what I say, Hannchen Gerber?"

Her head bobbed again, dutifully. He was positive she did not understand. Catching her by the shoulders, he held her away from him. "Look at me."

She lifted her face. The starlight shone on her tear-damp cheeks. The shadows filled her eyes.

"In time, you will understand," he said. "For now, you must accept. Is so."

Once more she nodded. But in a small voice, she said, "*Bitte* — please, you will not be keep here that Rosy woman. Yes?"

With a sigh, he replied, "We discuss it later. Perhaps tomorrow."

"*Danke!*" She threw her arms around his neck as if he had agreed to do as she asked. "*Ach, danke!*"

He started to push her away, wanting to make it clear to her that he had not agreed. He had no intention of sending Rosy away. He simply meant to stall Hannchen until she'd had time to know Rosy better and to learn just how helpful Rosy could be to her.

The sudden sound of a gunshot shattered the night stillness.

Aware of lead slamming into the ground not far away, Dutch grabbed Hannchen in his arms. He lunged back into the shadows against the house, dragging her with him.

She made a small strangling noise, as if a scream were trapped in her throat. He could feel her body trembling against his. Shoving her up to the wall of the house, he pressed himself in front of her.

His hand had gone automatically to his hip. But he wasn't wearing a gun. Flexing the empty hand, he scanned the woods.

Starlight touched the edges of the forest. A breeze played along the branches of the trees. The leaves fluttered, the light dancing on their tips. The wavering shadows were deep. He could see nothing within them. He caught the scent of burnt powder, but not the odor of a horse or a man.

Gripping Hannchen's arms, he sidled her along the wall toward the door. A lamp was burning in the kitchen. He knew that if he opened the door to shove Hannchen inside, they would both be silhouetted in the doorway. Perfect targets.

At the door, he halted and listened. He could hear no sounds at all from within the kitchen.

Where was Rosy, he wondered. Hadn't she heard the shot? He couldn't expect anything helpful from Claudia Prescott, but surely Rosy Tatum would be alerted by a gunshot. Surely she would want to know what was happening. If she were to come into the kitchen, he could call softly for her to put out the lamp. And bring him a gun.

But there were no sounds from the kitchen. And none from the woods.

There was no second shot. Perhaps because the person behind the gun couldn't draw a bead on Dutch and Hannchen as they crouched in the shadows. Or perhaps whoever fired that one shot had slunk back into the darkness to run. Perhaps there was no more danger waiting in the shadows now.

Cautiously, Dutch reached out. Holding his body pressed against the wall beside the doorway, he gave the latch a quick jerk and slammed open the door. Lamplight filled the sudden opening.

His move startled Hannchen. It broke the grip of her terror. Her voice escaped her throat in a scream. She flung herself toward the doorway.

He snatched at her. His fingers caught the cloth of her sleeve. It ripped. For a moment she was framed against the light as she lunged through the doorway into the kitchen.

From within the house, Dutch heard a scurry of sound. Claudia Prescott hadn't responded to the gunshot, but now she was answering Hannchen's scream, calling to the girl as she hurried toward the kitchen.

They met just inside. Dutch saw their shadows cross the open doorway. Hannchen's screams turned to sobs, and Claudia's voice murmured in comfort for the girl. Neither seemed aware of the danger that might still wait outside.

They were both fools, he thought angrily. Lucky fools. There was no second shot.

He told himself that the person with the gun might be waiting for him to show himself.

Standing motionless in the shadows next to the doorway, he called softly to the women inside, "Put out the light!"

The lamp continued to glow brightly.

They were worse than fools. They were useless. Where was Rosy?

He tried calling again, "Put out the light!"

A moment passed without response. Then Claudia shouted back at him, "Mr. Falke! What's happened? What have you done to this child?"

He realized from her voice that she was about to step into the open doorway. He snapped at her, "Stay back!"

At the same time, Hannchen screeched, "*Nein*, Frau Prescott! Savages! Wild Indians!"

"Nonsense," Claudia answered, stepping into the doorway, framing herself against the bright lamplight. She leaned out. "Mr. Falke?"

No one shot her.

Dutch felt almost disappointed. If she had been shot, it would have been no more than she deserved for her stupidity. From the darkness, he growled at her, "Put out the light!"

"Why?"

"*Hear me! Put out the light!*"

"Well, of all the —" She went back into the kitchen. At last the light went out.

He eased inside and pulled the door shut behind him. Another lamp was glowing in the living room. Enough of its light spilled into the kitchen to show him Hannchen standing with her face pressed into her hands as she cried. He shoved past her.

Claudia followed him, insisting, "Mr. Falke, I must have an explanation!"

Ignoring her, he strode across the living room. His gun belt was hanging from a peg near the front door. As he reached for it, he saw that the holster was empty.

With a grunt of surprise, he turned and looked at Claudia. "Where is Rosy Tatum?"

"How should I know?" she said indignantly. "I am hardly to be held accountable for the whereabouts of your servants. I have been in the bedroom since dinner. What is happening here? Poor Hannchen is in a state of terror! What did you do to her?"

"You did not hear the gunshot?"

"Gunshot?"

"Yes. A loud noise. Bang! You did not hear such a noise? You did not wonder at it?"

She looked at him as if he insulted her by asking such idiotic questions. Giving a shrug, she said, "Mr. Falke, your behavior is strange, to say the least!"

It was useless trying to talk to her. With a sigh, he turned away and shouted, "Rosy Tatum!"

No answer.

He lifted a rifle from the rack. As he was checking the load, the door flew open. Rosy came dashing in. Her face was flushed and she was gasping as if she had been running hard. She had Dutch's revolver in her hand.

Scowling at the gun, he said sharply, "Where have you been?"

Her eyes opened very wide as they met his. She held the gun out to him. Breathlessly, she replied, "I heard a shot!"

"So?"

"I tooken your gun and went outside to see what was wrong."

"By the back of the house, the shot was fired. I myself was there. I did not see you."

"I didn't want whoever was shooting to get his sights on me. I came out the front. I circled around through the woods."

"Did you see anyone?"

She shook her head.

"Mr. Falke!" Claudia interrupted. "I demand an explanation!"

Wheeling to face her, he leveled the revolver at her. "Go away! Go, take Fräulein Gerber and make her calm. Tell her it is not Indians. Go!"

"Well, I never — !" She glowered at the gun, then spun on her heel and stalked off to collect Hannchen. The girl was still sobbing as Claudia herded her into the bedroom and slammed the door behind them.

Dutch turned back to Rosy. "What are you think?"

"About what?"

"Who shot at me?"

She gave a slow, thoughtful shake of her head, as if she could come up with no suggestions.

"One of your brothers?"

"Oh, no!"

"Then who?"

"Maybe somebody's mad at you, Mr. Falke. What about that Quint Leslie feller who you said wants to put his cattle across the river onto your land? You reckon maybe he would have tooken a shot at you?"

"If he did, he would not miss so."

126

"Maybe he only meant to scare you."

Dutch doubted that. Quint Leslie knew him well enough to know a simple shot in the night wouldn't spook him.

He thought of James Easton. Who the hell was Easton? What did he want around Falcon range? Easton seemed to be damned interested in the women. Certainly Claudia Prescott could hold no charm for him. Had he taken a fancy to Hannchen? Did he mean to have her for himself, even if it meant killing Dutch from ambush?

Dutch shook his head at the thought. Easton didn't seem the kind for such a foolish trick. He wondered if Easton really was interested in Hannchen, or if perhaps there was something he wanted from Dutch that he believed he might get by working through Hannchen.

Or was Rosy wrong about her brothers? Had it been one of them there in the shadows?

Puzzled, Dutch returned the revolver to its holster. He asked Rosy, "You are finished now with the work in the kitchen?"

"Just about."

"My shoulder is still sore. Before you are go to bed, you are again rub away the ache for me?"

"I'd be right pleased." She smiled at him. Then she glanced toward the door to the bedroom Claudia and Hannchen were sharing. She commented, "That Hannchen of yours is a real crybaby, ain't she?"

He had to allow to himself that she was right about that.

CHAPTER
TEN

As usual, Dutch woke well before sunup. The house was silent. He supposed none of the women were awake yet. Dressed, he made his way through the darkness to the kitchen. When he had poked up the embers in the stove, he set a pot of coffee to cook. Then he headed out to tend the horses.

With most of the saddle stock out on roundup, there wasn't much work to be done at the barn. The sun hadn't yet showed itself when he finished. The soft dawn glow didn't give enough light for him to investigate the woods for sign of that prowler the night before. He filled a bucket with fresh water for the kitchen and returned to the house.

As he swung around it to enter from the back, he saw lamplight glowing through a kitchen window. There was a pleasant smell of side meat frying. He grinned with anticipation as he walked in.

Rosy was busy at the stove. The coffee he had started was boiling merrily. Giving him a bright good morning, Rosy grabbed a cup and poured it full for him.

As he accepted it, he asked, "Are the others up yet?"

Claudia and Hannchen had chosen to share a bedroom. That had left the other empty room for Rosy.

She told him, "I don't think so. Their door was closed when I come by it. I reckon them high-toned kind of ladies sleep later than working folk. I reckon I slept a mite late myself. I didn't waken until I heard stirring in the house. I should've been up in time to have that coffee ready for you. I will be, tomorrow."

She had a good ear if she had heard him stirring, he thought. An ear like a creature of the forest. She had some of the quality of a forest animal about her, a quick alertness that pleased him.

She said, "You ain't got no hens, have you, Mr. Falke?"

"No." He seated himself at the table across from the stove and sipped the hot coffee.

"You ought to," she told him. "Fresh eggs is good for breakfast. I know a dozen ways to fix them. And a body needs fresh eggs to make good pancakes. I'd 've made you some this morning, only there ain't no eggs. I got fry and taters and biscuits and the rest of last night's pie for you. What else you want?"

"That will be enough."

"You think it'll suit them ladies?" She used the word *ladies* as if it were an insult.

"I suppose so," he answered, certain it wouldn't suit Claudia Prescott. He didn't think anything would.

Rosy was doubtful, too. "They didn't seem to think much of the vittles I set out yesterday. That English lady didn't like none of them at all."

"There was no tea," he said sarcastically. "Today you are go into town and buy tea."

"Me? Go into town?" The idea seemed to surprise and please her.

"We are all go. You are buy what is needed for the kitchen, for to cook what you wish. Whatever you need."

Her eyes shone at the idea of stocking the kitchen to suit herself. As she turned to the stove, she said, "I'd be real pleasured."

He sat watching her work as the sun came up, spilling its long light through the window. Her biscuits baked to a golden brown. Still there was no sign of Hannchen or Claudia.

"Should I ought to go call them to breakfast?" Rosy asked Dutch as she took the biscuits from the oven.

"No."

"But these vittles is all ready."

"You and I will eat them. The others will eat what is left when they are come."

"The vittles will be cold by then. It won't do them no good to get warmed over."

"If the women cannot rise in time for breakfast, they can eat cold biscuits. Come. Sit. We eat now." Dutch gestured for her to join him at the kitchen table.

She was good company, he thought as they ate and chatted together. He asked her, "Can you read?"

She gave a sad shake of her head. "I can figure accounts, though, and count money. There can't any shopkeeper chouse me out of a penny. Pa learned me counting. He learned it to us all. He couldn't learn us to read, though. He ain't no hand at that himself."

"There are no school where you come from?"

130

"It was an awful long piece off and not much ways none of us could get to it but now and then. Our place was way back off in the high hills. Not much of anything around but hills. We hardly even had a trace of a road. It wasn't easy for us to get a crop down to the market. When we had a crop."

"You are farmers?"

"Uh huh. Pa said it was all right when he was young on account of back then a body didn't need much in the way of money. Most everything a body needed could be growed right there on the farm. He could trade for the rest. But it got to where, with taxes and all, a body had to bring in a money crop regular. And the land begun to wear out. Each year, the crop was worse than before. Finally, we couldn't hardly grow nothing but weeds, and they did poorly. So we packed up and come to the West looking for new land."

She leaned toward him, as if sharing a very important bit of news with him. "You know, there's land for the taking out here, if you can find it!"

He nodded. "Homestead land."

"Only trouble is, first you got to find a piece of it that's fit to have and somebody else ain't squatted on it already. Then you got to have money to get started on it. Gov'ment wants you to pay down and take papers if you mean to keep it. You got to build a house and have seed and tools to start up. About all we got is some wore-out old tools."

"You do not have the money or the seed?"

"We had some when we started. We figured we had enough when we left home. We got out onto the prairie where there's a mess of land. Too much of it. The land was good enough and we got set and took papers and built us a house and got crops in and everything, just like we'd been hoping. It looked like life was gonna be just fine for us. Then the wind come up. It come roaring in without a hill or a tree on the whole prairie to slow it down. Come a twister, a big fierce old wind turning all around and around as it come." She gestured with her hands, showing him the violence of the tornado. "It blowed everything away. Crops and house and all. It didn't hardly leave us nothing. So we packed up and moved on. That old prairie ain't no good to live on nohow."

"Why not?"

"There ain't nothing there. Nothing but nothing, no matter which way you look. It drives a body crazy just looking off at nothing in every direction. A body needs hills and trees and a piece of water big enough to drop a bucket into. Them prairie cricks run in the spring but they dry up in the summer to where they ain't hardly nothing at all."

"So you came here?"

"We figured to find us some hill country like we left back home. Folks told us there was way bigger hills to the west than ever we seen back home. We don't need no bigger hills, though. Just a nice piece of land like you got around here. You know, Mr. Falke, you're an awful lucky man. You got a real fine piece of land here. These hills and woods and cricks are every bit as purty as the ones back home."

"So you would like to take land here?"

"We'd like to. But folks in town told us the open land hereabouts was all claimed by the cowmen, and if we tried to put a plow to it, the cowmen would up and hang us all." She had been looking at him as she spoke. Suddenly she lowered her eyes. Color flushed her cheeks.

He could guess why. He said, "They told you I have hanged farmers for trying to settle on my land?"

She gave a small self-conscious nod. Then she met his eyes again. "But that just don't seem so, Mr. Falke. You don't seem to me like somebody who'd just up and do a thing like that. Not lynch poor folk without you gave them no chance. You been awful decent with my brothers and me."

He started to reply, but stopped and gestured for Rosy's silence. She heard the same distant sounds that he had. Silently, she shaped a word with her lips. "Horses?"

He nodded. Rising, he went into the living room. Rosy followed him, watching with apprehension as he pulled a rifle from the rack by the door and checked the loads in it.

The horses sounded to be headed toward the house. Through an open window, Dutch spotted them. Three riders out in the pasture, heading toward the house at a gallop. The set of Dutch's shoulders eased as he recognized Rosy's brothers.

As they came closer, one shouted a halloo to the house. The others joined in, shouting as if for the fun of it.

Dutch started for the door.

A scream from behind him spun him around. He jerked up the rifle, his finger on the trigger.

The door of the women's bedroom flew open. Claudia came dashing out. She was in her nightgown, her hair in a ruffled nightcap. She demanded of Dutch, "What is happening? We are being attacked?"

"Attacked?" he grunted, surprised by the word.

"The Indians," Claudia said, looking at the gun he held as if it confirmed her fears. "Have you enough weapons to stand them off?"

The clatter of hoofs outside stopped. Wade Tatum called, "Halloo the house!"

Frowning, Claudia turned to peer out the window. "That's not an Indian!"

"Is the hired men," Dutch said, understanding that the women had taken the sounds of galloping horses and the shouts to mean the house was under attack.

Claudia sighed with relief. Collecting herself, she said sharply, "They make an exceedingly uncivilized lot of noise." Then she took Hannchen by the arm and explained to the girl in German.

Hannchen was crying, insisting that she had seen the Indians as well as heard them. She stammered about wild red men with burning eyes and teeth like wolves and huge knives meant to strip away scalps.

"Alpdrücken," Dutch suggested. "She has the nightmare."

Holding and comforting the girl, Claudia glared at him. "Well, it's no wonder! That shooting last night and your abominable behavior and now all this bedlam! It's no wonder the poor child is frightened out of her wits!"

"I have told you here there are not wild Indians now," Dutch said stiffly.

"We lack suitable grounds upon which to give credence to your statements, Mr. Falke," she answered. "Your behavior has hardly been that of a gentleman. Those galloping horses, the shouting — that is a terrible way to be awakened in a strange place!"

"If at a decent hour you get up, the men would not be waking you." He turned his back to her. Jerking open the door, he stepped outside.

Rosy followed him out.

The three Tatum brothers sat their horses in front of the house. They had the mounts Dutch had sent them to the roundup camp for. Wade's old army saddle was on a full-chested bay gelding that was lathered under the reins and around the saddle.

"Morning, boss!" Wade grinned at Dutch. He dismounted and gave the bay a pat on the withers. "Now, that's a horse!"

Grinning in agreement, Rob stepped down. His horse was another bay, also heavily lathered. Threads of foam hung from its mouth.

Stony had no saddle. He rode a gunny sack tied onto the back of a chunky buckskin. He slid down and faced Dutch.

"You have run the horses," Dutch said harshly.

Wade kept on grinning. "They been running us! Them's a handful of horses. Stony come off his three times!"

"You come off yours once," Stony said. "And you got a saddle."

"Well, man! That's a bronco! One of them real hell-to-leather broncos the cowboys all talk about!" Wade answered proudly.

Scowling, Dutch touched the lathered neck of Wade's mount. Seeing his disapproval, Rob asked, "We done something wrong?"

"You run these horses without need," Dutch told him. "You make them tired. These horses must work. It is not good for them to run and be tired without need."

Wade's grin weakened but he hung on to it as he protested, "Hell, it don't hurt none to run the kinks out a horse. It's been a long time since the three of us was astride any decent horseflesh as could give a man a real ride."

Dutch knew the joy of racing a good horse, but men and horses both had to be disciplined if they were to serve a purpose. Both had to be used efficiently. Not misused. He said sharply, "Unsaddle the horses and rub them down. Do not water until they be cool. Do not run them again unless there is good cause. If one of these horses is become injured or foundered, the man who is done it will pay very much."

Wade's grin disappeared. He glared at Dutch with an obvious urge to strike out.

Rosy read his expression. "Mind now, Wade!"

"Let *him* mind!" Wade snapped. "I don't belong to him! I don't take his kind of talk off nobody!"

"Then you are not work for me," Dutch said.

136

"Then I don't work for you!" Grabbing a stirrup, Wade started to swing up onto the bay's back.

"And you are not ride *my* horse!" Dutch still had the rifle in his hand. He leveled it at Wade.

"Stop it!" Rosy shouted. "Both of you, stop it! Wade, you simmer down. You know you got a debt to Mr. Falke! You can't just up and quit on him!"

"I'll find some way to pay him," Wade said darkly. "I ain't gonna work for him!"

"What about you?" She looked to the other brothers.

They glanced at each other. Rob licked his lips thoughtfully. With reluctant loyalty, he replied, "I'll stick with Wade."

Stony put a hand on his mount's neck where the lather from the reins was drying into a salty crust.

"This here horse is right het up," he said, his eyes asking Wade to reconsider.

Wade hesitated.

Silently, Rosy pleaded with him. Her hand touched Dutch's arm lightly, asking him to yield a little if Wade would do as much.

Dutch spoke to Wade. "In this country, a horse can mean a man's life. A man must for his horse care as he is care for his life. This horse needs care."

He reached for the bay's bridle as if he meant to take the horse from Wade.

Wade tugged the reins, backing the bay. As he did it, he swung a leg over the horse's rump. Stepping to the ground, he said, "*I'll* tend him."

He wheeled stiffly. His head was held high in defense of his pride and self-respect. His stance defied anyone to accuse him of backing down.

Rob and Stony exchanged relieved looks. As Wade headed for the barn, Rob followed. Pausing, Stony mumbled, "I can't unsaddle. I ain't got no saddle to unsaddle with."

"In the barn should be an old saddle." Dutch started after Wade and Rob.

Rosy grabbed his arm. "I want to talk to you, Mr. Falke. Please!"

He told Stony, "Go ahead. In a minute, I come."

Once Stony was out of earshot, Rosy said softly to Dutch, "Just give them a little time. Let them talk to each other. Let Wade simmer down. They'll be all right."

"Do you think I am not be reasonable with them?" he asked her.

"No — not exactly. Only you got a hard way about you. You make the things you say sound kind of — uh — mean."

"This is a hard world, Rosy Tatum. A man must be hard or it can destroy him."

"*Hard* maybe," she allowed. "But he don't have to be *mean* about it."

He eyed her askance. "You think I am be mean?"

"You sort of act like it sometimes. People got feelings. You just now acted like you worry more over them horses of yours than over people."

"A man's life can be depend on his horse."

"It can depend on people, too."

138

A corner of his mouth quirked slightly. "I am rather trust my life to a horse than to a man."

She looked surprised. "Why?"

"A horse is never ask where a man is born or make mock of the way he speaks. A horse is not take advantage of a boy's ignorance and steal all he has, or curse him for a dirty foreigner." He turned away from her. Glancing at the rifle he still held, he added, "A horse is not from ambush shoot at a man."

She offered no reply.

There was no good in brooding over the long past, he told himself. The present and the future were what mattered. He should be about this day's business.

CHAPTER
ELEVEN

Dutch hitched up the surrey while the women had breakfast and prepared themselves for the trip into town. By the time they finally came out to the surrey, Hannchen seemed to have forgotten her scare.

She had dressed herself in a suit of pale blue that set off the blue of her eyes. There were ruffles of white lace at her throat, pinned with a cameo in a setting of gold. Her face glowed with excitement. Her mouth pursed in a small inward smile.

Looking at her, Dutch could understand why Herr Onkel Heinrich had chosen her. The Americans had a phrase that described her perfectly. Something about being like a china doll. She would make a beautiful bride, he thought as he helped her into the surrey. But the thought did not cheer him.

The prospect of the trip into town had not improved Claudia Prescott. She was dressed in a suit of severe dark gray, and the look of stern disapproval she gave Dutch when he boosted her into the surrey was just as severe.

Rosy had no change of clothing, but she had done her best to prepare herself for the trip. Her face was scrubbed and her eyes glowed with joy that was different from Hannchen's look of pleasure. Rosy's smile was turned outward, shining as brightly on Dutch as the morning sun.

As Rosy stepped up to the surrey, Claudia scowled at her. "Have you no shoes, child?"

For the flash of an instant, Rosy's face paled. The joy in her eyes dimmed as if a cloud had passed before their sun. Dutch could see her embarrassment and felt an urge to defend her.

She answered Claudia for herself. "The Blessed Lord made my feet. If they're good enough for Him, they're sure good enough for me."

With a harrumph, Claudia turned to Dutch. "If this girl is to serve in the house, she will *have* to have suitable attire."

"We will get it for her," he said, taking Rosy's hand to help her into the surrey. He felt her fingers cling to his a moment before they withdrew.

The old buzzard had frightened her, he thought. No, not frightened. It would take a good deal more than a few harsh words to frighten Rosy Tatum. But Claudia's words had hurt the girl. Rosy, in her tatters, was every bit as proud as Hannchen in her finery and Claudia Prescott in her incomprehensible private world.

Well, Rosy would have clothes to fit her pride, he told himself as he took his seat in the surrey. She would have shoes and a dress from the mercantile shelf, and fabric to make more for herself if she wished.

He would not allow her to suffer embarrassment because of her poverty while she was working for him.

141

He wouldn't have that damned old buzzard picking at her just because the girl had been born to hard times.

It was late morning when they reached town. At the mercantile, Dutch arranged for the women to charge their purchases to the Falcon account. Leaving them there, he collected the surrey and headed for the preacher's house to make the wedding arrangements.

Parson Dowling lived in a clapboard cottage behind a white picket fence at a distance from the town. When Dutch drew up at the gate, Mrs. Dowling was on her knees in the yard, weeding her flower garden. Rising, she wiped her face with the back of one gloved hand and looked curiously at him.

He called a good morning to her from the seat of the surrey.

"Good morning, Mr. Falke," she replied. As the parson's wife, she had social obligations. She shaped up a polite little smile for him. "Won't you step down? Come on in and visit for a while?"

He climbed from the surrey and gave the tie line a hitch around the gatepost. There were chickens scratching in the yard. As he opened the gate to enter, he glanced at them and remembered that Rosy wanted some laying hens.

"It's been too long since I've seen you, Mr. Falke," Mrs. Dowling said, her tone making it clear that she felt he should attend church services far more regularly than he did. "What brings you here today? Not trouble at the ranch, I hope."

142

"Is business," he answered, his voice too sharp. Her unctuous manner was chafing at his already taut nerves. "Is at home Parson Dowling?"

"I'm afraid not. He's gone to call on Ben Riley. Mr. Riley's laid up with the ague, you know. But he should be back before long. Won't you come in and wait? I can make some tea."

He had taken his hat off to her. He fingered at the brim. He had been hoping to get this over with quickly. He sure as hell didn't want to sit around in the parlor trying to make conversation with this woman while he waited for her husband.

"I call again later."

She eyed him with obvious curiosity. "Perhaps I might help. You know, I work very closely with the parson. I help him prepare his sermons and I visit the sickly and give counsel to those in need. Perhaps you should discuss this matter with me. Sometimes a woman's viewpoint can be very helpful."

Apparently she was hoping he would confide some serious personal problem to her. Something that would make a juicy bit of gossip she could share with her friends.

He started to turn away.

She grabbed his arm. "If you'll just confide in me — !"

He thought of molasses, all sticky and clinging. Jerking away from her hand, he snapped, "I come back later!"

Her smile slipped. She forced it into place again. It was stiff and weak, barely able to cover her indignant disappointment. "If you wish."

"Yes," he grunted, striding to the surrey. She stood watching him as he stepped aboard and lifted reins. He stopped and turned to her again. "Would you be sell some chickens?"

"Chickens?" She frowned in puzzlement.

"Yes. Hens. To lay eggs."

Her eyes widened with incredulity. "Is *that* what you came to discuss with my husband?"

Impulsively, he replied, "Yes."

From the way she stared at him, he knew she would soon be telling her friends about the visit from the strange Dutchman with his peculiar foreign ways. She would say that he certainly behaved like a man with many black deeds on his conscience. Very odd behavior for a man who simply wanted to buy some hens. She would shake her head and cluck over his ruination as if she were an old hen herself.

"Well, yes, I suppose I might sell some if the price is right," she said.

"I need hens and a rooster."

"You're not planning to go into the business, are you?"

He shook his head.

"Tending chickens for the table is woman's work," she said, hoping he would admit something of interest in reply.

"I come back for them later." He bit his words short, his tone telling her that he did not intend to say more. Giving her a curt nod of goodbye, he set his team into a trot.

As he drove back toward town, he was aware that she stood gazing after him, wondering about his behavior.

He was a little puzzled by his actions himself. There was no reason not to tell the parson's wife that he wanted to plan a wedding. After all, she would find out as soon as he had spoken to the parson. Word would spread through the town quickly enough then.

Hell, it had probably already spread. Quint Leslie had known about it the same evening that the women arrived in Newt's Ford.

How had Quint known? he wondered. The only one he had told was Slim Walker, and Slim could be trusted to keep his mouth shut.

It occurred to Dutch that there were two other people in town that day who knew. Claudia Prescott and Hannchen herself. But he didn't think either of them had met Quint Leslie. Neither of them had much opportunity to talk to any of the townsfolk between their arrival and his meeting with them. Yet Quint had known just a short time later.

There was one person with whom the women had talked at length. The stranger, James Easton. If Quint Leslie had learned about the planned wedding from Easton in such a short time, it seemed unlikely that Easton was a stranger to Quint.

That meant Dutch had business with James Easton. Now.

He rattled the surrey into town, jerking it to a halt in front of the coach house. He was hoping that Easton was staying there. And that Easton was in his room.

As he stepped down from the surrey, he heard Rosy Tatum calling his name. She sounded excited. He wheeled toward her.

"What is?" he asked as she ran up to him.

Breathless, she said, "It's your Hannchen!"

"What about her?"

"We've lost her!"

"What?"

"We've lost her!" Rosy repeated. "One minute she was right there with us in the store, and the next thing we knew, she was gone, and now we can't find her nowhere!"

"Whoa!" he said, aware of the staring eyes and eager ears of the people on the walk nearby. He gestured for her to follow him into the office of the coach house.

The clerk behind the desk looked up as they entered. Dutch drew Rosy into a corner near the door and spoke too softly for the clerk to catch his words. "Now, tell me just what has happen."

Rosy matched her tone to his. "Them two and me was in the mercantile. The counterjumper was with Mrs. Prescott and your Hannchen, and I was just sort of poking around, looking at all the do-pretties, and your Hannchen went off to the outhouse. Mrs. Prescott come to help me pick out a right nice sort of dress for to wear to work at your house, and some shoes."

She tugged up her skirt and thrust a foot at him. "See! Ain't they nice!"

Automatically, he glanced at the foot. It was clad in a high-topped side-buttoned shoe of soft black kid. He said, "Yes, very nice. But about Hannchen?"

"They're kind of tight. Mrs. Prescott says they'll break in all right though."

"About Hannchen?" he persisted.

"After a while we figured it was past time she ought to 've come back, so Mrs. Prescott went to look for her. She found the outhouse door open and there wasn't nobody inside. Not no sign of your Hannchen at all!" She looked at him with an expression of dismay.

He thought he saw a glitter in her eyes that didn't fit the expression. Sternly, he said, "Where is Hannchen?"

"Gone! We done looked in all the stores up and down the street. She ain't in none of them. Mrs. Prescott went off to find the town marshal and tell him. I was going back behind the stores to look in all the outhouses when I seen you coming into town. You looked in a right hurry, Mr. Falke. Did you know something was wrong?"

"Rosy," he said, anger edging his voice. *"Where is she?"*

"I don't know!"

He put a hand on her arm, his fingers closing tightly around it just above the elbow. "Rosy, you are glad she is gone. Last night, when you are take that shot with my gun, are you shoot at me or at Hannchen?"

"What!" Her face filled with surprise. And with guilty fear.

"Last night, you fire that shot. You use my revolver. You are not replacing the empty cartridge before I take back the gun from you."

She shook her head in denial.

"Do not lie to me, Rosy Tatum. There is only one shot. You are outside with my gun. This morning before I put on the gun, I check it. I find one spent round."

"You must've shot it off sometime yourself and forgot!"

"When I use the gun, afterward I always clean it and replace empty rounds. I always check it before I put it on. I do not forget when I use it." His grip on her arm tightened as he spoke.

"You must've! I didn't do it!" She squirmed against his grip.

"Rosy . . ."

"I didn't! I — I — oh, Mr. Falke! I didn't shoot *at* nobody at all!" she said with misery, avoiding his eyes.

"Then why are you take my gun and fire it last night?"

"Only just to scare *her*."

"To scare Hannchen?"

She nodded.

"Why?"

"On account of she's only just a fluffy little kitten and she ain't no good for — for — for no life like out here. She wouldn't be of no use to you on your ranch, Mr. Falke. Not when she's all the time bawling and going all spooky about nothing like a loco horse. I only just wanted you to see for yourself what she's really like!"

"So you are frighten her and now she is run away!"

"No." She gave a slow shake of her head. "Your Hannchen ain't up and run away, Mr. Falke. Not her! She wouldn't run away alone. Not when she's afraid

148

there's wild Indians behind all the bushes. She wouldn't go out of hollering distance of Mrs. Prescott by her lonesome. Not of her own free will, she wouldn't!"

That was true, he thought. Through his teeth, he muttered, "Easton!"

"What?"

Turning from Rosy, he strode to the desk. The clerk was watching him. He asked, "Is there stay here a man named James Easton?"

"Yes."

"His room is where?"

The clerk hesitated. Dutch's eyes on him were harshly demanding. He gave in to them and said, "Up the stairs to your right at the end of the hall. But he ain't up there now."

"Where is he?"

"How should I know?"

Dutch gave a grunt of angry disgust. He turned back to Rosy. "You say that the Englishwoman is gone to see Sam Steele?"

The name didn't register with her. She said, "She went looking for the town marshal."

"Damn!" he muttered, shoving open the coach house door. On the walk, he hurried toward Sam Steele's office.

Rosy had to scurry to keep up with his stride. A sadness edged her voice as she asked him, "You really are worried about her, ain't you? You really do want her for a wife?"

"I would be happy if she be back in Hesse," he admitted. "But she is here now. She is my responsibility."

"So you mean to go ahead and marry her, no matter what?"

"It is promised. The word is given."

Rosy said nothing more.

The town marshal's office was a small frame building elbowed in between a pair of high false fronts. The door was closed. Dutch slammed it open.

Inside, Claudia Prescott was seated on a stiff wooden settle. She dabbed at her eyes with a tiny square of white linen.

Sam Steele hovered over her. He was saying, "All right! All right! I'll go look for her. But I tell you, you're all het up over nothing. She'll show up soon enough."

Leaning to one side, away from Sam Steele's breath, Claudia gasped, "She won't! Something terrible has happened to her! I know it has! I knew all along that it was wrong to bring that poor innocent child to this savage country! Whigs and common mechanics and filthy peasants! It's your duty to find her, Mr. Steele! You have to —"

She stopped short as Dutch stalked into the office. Sam wheeled away from her. He looked at Dutch with mournfully woebegone eyes.

Dutch growled at him, "You do not be concerned for the girl. I am take care of her. By me is the responsibility!"

Claudia peered at him over her handkerchief. "You have hardly done a very good job of being responsible for her, Mr. Falke!"

Sam gestured at Claudia. "I been trying to tell her that there ain't nothing to worry about."

Dutch gave a nod as if he agreed.

Rising, Claudia confronted him. "The poor child is missing! Lost! Can't you understand that? She may be a victim of foul play! She may have been murdered — or worse!"

"Likely she's only just wandering around in the shops looking at all the geegaws," Sam said to Dutch in a put-upon whine. "You know how it is with women."

"We have already looked in all the shops for her!" Claudia said.

Sam insisted, "You must've missed seeing her."

Claudia harrumphed indignantly.

"Come," Dutch said to her.

She started to argue.

He glared at her. "Come!"

Scowling resentfully, she followed him onto the street. She didn't stop talking. "You are mistaken, Mr. Falke! Something terrible has happened to that poor child! Something terrible! I just know it!"

"If it is so," he growled, "Sam Steele is be no help."

Claudia looked morose, as if she concurred in that opinion. She demanded, "What are you going to do?"

"Find her."

Turning away from the women, he started toward the livery stable.

Rosy hurried after him.

Claudia hesitated, then, with her chin up and her expression grim, she followed.

CHAPTER
TWELVE

Tinker Jim was busy taking a wheel off a buggy when Dutch entered the stable yard. He had a heavy wrench on an axle nut and was leaning his weight against it. The nut seemed to be frozen. His face was red, dripping the sweat of his effort. He gave Dutch a quick glance over his shoulder and grunted, "What can I do for you this morning?"

"Is anyone hire from you today a rig or saddle horses?" Dutch asked.

Tinker Jim gave the nut another hard shove. It loosened. Slipping the wrench from it, he straightened up and turned to face Dutch. He noticed the women then.

Rosy was close behind Dutch, looking as if she expected trouble and intended backing him up when it came.

Claudia had stopped short at the edge of the stable yard. With one hand she held her skirts up clear of the dirt. Her other hand clung tightly to her reticule.

Bobbing his head, Tinker Jim greeted each woman in turn.

Dutch snapped impatiently, "Is someone hire a rig or horses today?"

The blacksmith set the big wrench down on the anvil. Moving with deliberate slowness, he wiped his hands. As if to clarify a difficult question for himself, he repeated Dutch's words.

"Well?" Dutch demanded.

Rosy spoke up. "It's awful important, mister."

Tinker Jim looked at her with a mockery of wide-eyed innocence. "Important, ma'am?"

"Yes!" Dutch said.

Turning to Dutch again, the smith twisted his face into a knot. "Well, now, let me think about it."

It was obvious that he was stalling. Dutch thought he sure as hell knew something he didn't want to admit. "Tell me!"

"It might be," Tinker Jim drawled slowly. "Renting out horses and rigs is my business. That and shoeing and —"

"*Tell me!*" Dutch's hands fisted at his sides.

Rosy edged up next to him. Her fingertips touched his arm lightly, the gesture asking that he restrain his growing anger.

Tinker Jim glanced at Dutch's fists. He scowled at the implied threat. "What the hell business is it of yours if I rent out horses?"

Claudia stepped forward, holding her skirts well away from the dirt and grease of the smithy. She held herself coldly aloof as she spoke, as if she deeply resented having to confide in a common tradesman. "Fräulein Hannchen Gerber has disappeared. We greatly fear that she has been taken against her will!"

154

A corner of Tinker Jim's mouth hinted at a grin as he replied, "I wouldn't say that. Not against her will. Oh no, ma'am, you shouldn't worry none about that!"

"What is?" Dutch demanded. "What are you know about this?"

The smith stood at least a head shorter than Dutch. He stiffened, making himself as tall as he could and glared defiantly. "Dutchman, you mind your own chickens. You leave young love go on its own way! You hear!"

Claudia asked, "What on earth do you mean by that?"

To herself, Rosy whispered, "She's done run off with somebody!"

"Then they *are* come here!" Dutch said. "From you they got horses or a rig. Which are they take? Where are they go from here?"

Side-stepping slightly, Tinker Jim moved a hand toward the wrench lying on the anvil. "Let them alone, Dutchman!"

"Where are they go? How are they travel, by horse or rig?" Dutch growled. "Answer me!"

The smith gave a shake of his head in refusal of a reply. His fingers closed on the wrench. He held it at his side as if it were a weapon.

Frightened, Rosy shoved between the two men. "Hold on! Hold on now!"

Claudia said, "Sir, you do not understand. Fräulein Gerber has been stolen away. We must find her before something terrible happens to her!"

155

"*You* don't understand, ma'am," Tinker Jim said with a grunting little laugh. "You got it all wrong. That little gal ain't been taken against her will. She's run off with the man that she's chose for herself. I don't mean to see no pretty little gal like her made to marry somebody she don't want to marry." He darted his eyes significantly toward Dutch. "I ain't letting this Dutchman step in and ruin that little gal's life for her. You understand?"

Dutch frowned. Whatever story Easton had given Tinker Jim had certainly convinced him. Hannchen must have been co-operative. Could she have gone willingly with Easton? Did she believe that Easton was in love with her and was taking her away to marry her? Would she rather marry a complete stranger than the man she had been sent to wed?

But perhaps Easton was less of a stranger to Hannchen than Dutch was. Easton had traveled in the same coach with Hannchen and Claudia. He had probably spent hours in conversation with them. All had stopped together at the way stations. Perhaps Easton had found moments to be alone with Hannchen, moments to ingratiate himself with her.

Just who was Easton? Some hireling Quint Leslie had sent for? It must have been luck that put Easton onto the same stagecoach as Hannchen. The Devil take Quint Leslie's luck!

Glaring at Tinker Jim, struggling against the anger of his impatience, Dutch said, "I must find the lady. If I be right, she has great danger. If I be wrong, I am not

156

interfere with her wishes. But I must find her. I must make certain."

Tinker Jim studied his face thoughtfully. "You swear that to me, Dutchman? You swear you won't interfere?"

"Yes."

"You won't stop her?"

"Not if it is her will to go," Dutch said.

Rosy nodded.

"All right," Tinker Jim said. "They got two saddle horses off me. Hired a sidesaddle for the lady. They told me that they was going to go straight out to the parson's place from here to tie the knot."

Dutch had been on the road and at the parsonage during the time Hannchen disappeared. He was sure he would have seen them if they had gone that way. So Easton had lied about where he was taking Hannchen.

He turned to Rosy. "You can drive the surrey, yes?"

She nodded.

"Then take it. Take back by the ranch Mrs. Prescott and wait there."

She looked as if she wanted to protest, but she nodded again, in acceptance of his orders.

"I take a horse," he said to Tinker Jim as he started for the barn.

The smith followed him inside. There were several horses in the stalls. The sorrel filly thrust its head over the gate to look at him.

The filly was a good horse, he thought. It might be a ladies' mount, but it had speed and bottom and was

157

trustworthy. He didn't know as much about any of the hacks that Tinker Jim offered for hire. He reached for the latch of the filly's stall.

"Hey, you can't take her!" Tinker Jim objected. "Sam Steele says that I got to hold her here until he gives me a release for her."

"If Sam Steele is make the trouble, tell him to come make it for me," Dutch grumbled as he led the filly from the stall.

Tinker Jim dutifully muttered more objections while he watched Dutch saddle up, but he didn't try to stop him.

Outside, Dutch located the hoofmarks of the horses Hannchen and Easton had ridden. They went into the alley paralleling the main street. Astride, he set out to follow them.

He was leaning from the saddle, studying the sign, when he heard a galloping horse approaching from behind. Straightening, he wheeled the filly and saw Stony Tatum racing toward him.

Rosy was behind her brother on his mount's rump. She shouted over Stony's shoulder, "Wait up a minute, Mr. Falke!"

Dutch gigged the filly and hurried to meet them. "What is? Is Quint Leslie make the move?"

"Yeah!" Stony answered breathlessly. His face was red under its coat of sweat-caked dust. He had ridden hard and fast. He paused to grab a breath. Then, waving one hand wildly, he spilled out a string of words.

158

"We seen them cows we been watching for! They're beginning to bunch them across the river just like you said they would! You want to come quick?"

Dutch licked his lips as he considered. Quint hadn't wasted any time. Which way to go? After Hannchen, or after the cattle?

Perhaps both lay in the same direction. If Quint had the girl, he might have her out there with the herd, where he could demonstrate that he held her hostage. If he put her in with the drive, she would be a shield against Dutch's guns.

"You got to come quick!" Stony was saying, his voice jerky and his eyes blinking rapidly. "They'll be starting across soon! You got to come!"

"You are send for Slim Walker as I ordered, yes?"

"Uh huh! Come on, Mr. Falke!"

"Rosy," Dutch said, "what you have done with the Englishwoman?"

"She's waiting in the surrey in front of the coach house. That's all as far as we had got when Stony come riding in looking for you."

"You go back, take her to the ranch. Take care of her, yes?"

Rosy looked as if she would much rather ride along with Dutch and take a hand in the trouble. He almost wished she could. He trusted her more than he did her brothers. But he couldn't ask her to go into danger. And whether he liked it or not, he was responsible for Claudia Prescott as well as for Hannchen Gerber.

"All right," Rosy sighed. She slid from the horse's rump and looked up at her brother. Her brow wrinkled.

159

"Stony, you sure you know what you're talking about?"

"Sure!" he snapped at her. "You shut up, sis, and do what you're told!" Almost as an afterthought, he added, "Before you get Mr. Falke mad at you."

She nodded.

Touching spurs to the filly's flanks, Dutch told Stony, "Come!"

Stony spun his mount and gigged it to catch up with Dutch.

Behind them, Rosy stood watching, her brow still pursed in a small frown.

Across the bridge, Stony led Dutch onto the trail that headed north parallel to the river. Dutch knew several places in that direction where a crossing might be made. Any of them could be defended well enough if the Falcon crew got there in time.

Again, he asked Stony, "You are sent for Slim Walker and the crew?"

Bobbing his head, Stony replied nervously, "Wade was gonna go after them the same time I left to come fetch you!"

Dutch wondered if he was frightened. He hoped he wouldn't have to rely on the Tatums in a fight. He had his doubts about any of them being of much use to him.

The trail they rode twisted through stands of heavy growth along the top of the bluff that flanked the river on the Falcon side. Across the river, on Quill land, much of the forest had been timbered out. Undergrowth had been cut away for access and trampled down by the

160

hoofs of work oxen. The ground was bare. The wind swept across rotting stumps.

Already, the face of the far bluff was being broken under the pounding of the weather. Deep gullies gashed down it. Pieces of the bluff had fallen away, dropping stumps into the water. Most of them were carried on downstream, but one big stump was hung up in a shallow. Mud and bits of drifting debris clung to it, building up around it. It was forming a barrier that was changing the flow of the river. The current, turning from the obstruction, was beginning to undercut the bluff on Dutch's side. Before long, it too would begin to crumble.

Riding past the stump, Dutch made a mental note to get it out before it could cause serious damage.

Beyond the land Quint Leslie had timbered out there was still some uncut forest, but hungry cattle hunting graze on the overstocked range were rapidly destroying the undergrowth, giving the woods a weak, sickly look.

The cut separating Quill land from Falcon range widened. The bluff turned away from the river on Dutch's side, leaving a broad flood plain bare to the sun. During the summer months the bottom land sprouted scattered growths of low brush and wild flowers. The trail forked, one branch working down the face of the bluff to the bottom plain while the other continued through the heavy brush and the woods atop the bluff.

Upstream, across the river, the bluff was low, with a slope to its face. Handled properly, cattle could be pushed down the slope into the water. They would have

161

a hard swim across the deep swift channel of the river, but the landing on the bare plain under the bluff on the Falcon side would be easy. And the plain was large enough for a good-sized bunch to be held on it.

Farther upstream, the cut narrowed again. There, a gap opened in the face of the bluff above the plain where an old stream had once made itself a bed down to join the river. Now the stream was almost dry. The bed was wide and open enough for cattle to be driven up it onto Dutch's range.

If Dutch let Quint Leslie get them across the river.

As he and Stony reached the fork of the trail, Stony drew rein. Pointing up across the river, he shouted, "Right over there! See them there!"

Halting, Dutch spotted the cattle massed within the thin forest across the river. He could hear the curses of the cowhands above the rumble of the rushing water. It looked as if they would be ready to start the drive across soon.

Stony had said Wade left to get the Falcon crew at the same time that Stony headed for town. Dutch figured Slim and the men should be on the way. It was possible they might arrive before Quint's men began to move the cattle into the water.

As he cocked an ear, hoping to catch some faint sound of galloping horses approaching, he glimpsed motion. Something was in the brush atop the bluff on the Falcon side of the river. Studying the spot, he saw a thin wisp of smoke rise from the brush to be lost in the breeze. Just a small puff such as might come from a cigarette.

He told Stony, "It is look like Quint has a scout on this side. Perhaps more than one."

Stony gave a start. "Where?"

Dutch pointed.

"That's where I left Rob!" Stony said. "He was gonna wait there for me to fetch you out!"

Perhaps it was only Rob Tatum, Dutch thought. Quint's men should be smart enough not to smoke while on a secret scout. But he didn't intend to take any chances. He drew his revolver as he gigged the filly onto the bluff-top trail.

Before reaching the stand of brush where he had seen the smoke, he reined in and dismounted. The filly wasn't trained to ground-hitch. He gave Stony the reins. "Wait here."

"What you gonna do?"

A good man didn't ask a lot of questions. He obeyed orders. Dutch didn't reply. Turning his back on Stony, he started up the trail afoot.

First he found a horse. It was tied to a bush and nibbling leaves. He recognized it as the one Rob Tatum had ridden. As he slipped silently past it, he caught the scent of smoke. Then he spotted the man with the cigarette.

Rob Tatum was hunkered in the brush near the edge of the bluff. He puffed at his quirley as he gazed lazily across the river. His rifle rested on his knees. He was totally unaware of anyone behind him until suddenly the muzzle of Dutch's revolver nudged him between the shoulder blades.

"Do not move," Dutch growled.

Rob gave a start that was almost a leap. The rifle slid from his knees. He jerked up his hands, gasping, "Don't shoot! Please don't shoot!"

Dutch withdrew the gun. He hoped that he had taught the poor fool a lesson in keeping watch.

Cautiously Rob looked back over his shoulder. He sucked breath between his teeth. There was no relief in his face at the sight of Dutch. His eyes were still filled with fear. "Oh, God! Please, Mr. Falke, it wasn't none of *my* doing! It was all Wade's idea! I was against it from the start!"

"Against what?" Dutch asked warily. As he spoke, he heard something crashing through the brush behind him. Wheeling, he pointed his gun toward the sound.

Stony came bulling through the bushes. He stopped short as he saw the revolver aimed at him. He had a long gun tucked under his arm. It fell to the ground as he flung his hands in the air.

"I tell you to wait!" Dutch snapped at him.

"I didn't mean no harm," he replied. "Honest, Mr. Falke! We didn't none of us mean no harm!"

"You are fools, both of you," Dutch said.

"Yes, sir," Stony agreed morosely. He looked as if he expected to be shot.

Dutch eyed him. "Why are you so fearful? What do you do that you think angers me?"

The brothers exchanged glances. Stony cleared his throat. "We — uh — Wade —"

"The gun!" Rob blurted. "That's it! When you stuck that gun in my back, I figured I must've done

164

something awful wrong! I didn't know what, but I sure as hell didn't mean to do it!"

"Uh huh," Stony mumbled. "I should've waited back there like you told me to."

Dutch supposed they had disobeyed his orders in other ways, too. He hoped none was serious. With a sigh, he said, "If Quint Leslie did have scouts by this side of the river, you would both be captured by now."

"Yes, sir," Stony agreed.

Evidently Quint hadn't bothered to send out scouts. Dutch thought Quint must feel very sure of himself — as he would if he was holding Hannchen as a hostage.

Lowering the gun, he asked Stony, "What are you do with the horses?"

"I left 'em with Rob's horse back there."

"You tied the filly?"

"Yes, sir."

He was relieved Stony'd had sense enough to do that much. Turning to Rob, he asked, "What happens across the river while you are watching?"

Rob licked his lips. Slowly he said, "Men over there been bunching up a lot of cattle. That's all I seen."

"Are you see a woman with them?"

"A woman?" Rob shook his head.

Dutch pushed past him to have a look at the far bank for himself. The Quill men had several large bunches among the trees. The cattle fretted nervously as if they knew they were going to be shoved over the bluff into the water. He counted a dozen riders working them.

Two more riders were back in the shadows at a distance from any cattle. Although he could not see

165

them clearly, Dutch was certain one must be Hannchen. The other didn't appear to be Quint Leslie. He guessed it was Easton at her side.

He couldn't pick out Quint among the riders working the cattle. The lanky man bossing the operation was Quint's foreman, Rudd Bigelow. Where was Quint, he wondered.

Easing back from the edge of the bluff, he told the Tatums, "Your brother should soon come with my crew. When they are here, tell my foreman I say to keep the cattle from Falcon range. Shoot cattle if it is necessary. But only shoot cattle. Not men. Not unless they be forced to do so. Understand?"

Stony nodded.

Rob said, "You ain't gonna be here when they come?"

"I must go across the river." As he spoke, Dutch stripped off his coat. He figured he could swim across unseen if he went well upstream of the herd. A cow or horse might not be able to climb the steep bluffs upriver, but a man could. He hoped he could circle through the woods and get the drop on Easton from behind. With luck, he could get Hannchen away safely before the Quill riders could be alerted.

It would take a lot of luck.

As he folded the coat and shoved it under a bush, he said, "I must take away from them the woman before there is danger to her."

"What woman you talking about?" Stony asked.

"My Hannchen."

"She's over there with them?"

166

Dutch nodded. "Quint Leslie is take her and hold her hostage."

"Damn! I don't like that!" Stony turned to address Rob. "I don't like that none at all!"

Dutch started to speak but stopped as he heard the rustling of leaves and cracking of twigs nearby. Men were coming on foot. Slim and the crew, he thought. But he hadn't heard horses.

A sense of wrongness sent his hand toward the gun on his hip. As his fingers reached it, the muzzle of a rifle thrust through the brush, pointing at him. A harsh voice snapped, "Hold it, Dutchman!"

Quint Leslie stepped out of the bushes with the rifle in his hand and a grin spread across his face. Wade Tatum was close behind him. Wade leveled the gun he carried at Dutch.

Stony and Rob both eased away from Dutch toward their brother.

Gazing at Quint's gun, with his own hand not quite around the butt of his revolver, Dutch realized that Wade had never gone for the Falcon crew at all. Wade had sold out to Quint Leslie. Stony and Rob were party to the betrayal. That was why they had been so spooky.

"I don't want to kill you, Dutchman," Quint was saying. His eyes gleamed with the pride of a conqueror. He wanted his opponent alive and aware of defeat. He went on smugly, "I don't want anything to happen to that little Dutch lady of yours, either."

"Then turn her loose," Dutch said. "Send her back safe to town."

167

"I will! I'll turn you both loose once I've got my herd on Falcon range and won our bet. Then you can go any damned place you want. Until then, I'll keep both of you nice and safe where you won't neither one get hurt. Not if you behave. Take off that gun belt."

Dutch made no move to obey.

Quint didn't like being defied. His grin faded. "I don't want to *kill* you, Dutchman, but I wouldn't mind *hurting* you a bit. If I put a bullet into, say, your leg, it'd bust the bone for sure. Maybe cripple you up for the rest of your life." He gave a nod toward the far bank. "As to that little Dutchie over there, my men got strict orders not to let her get hurt. But I can change them orders. If I was to say it, she'd get to ride into the river with the lead cattle. How do you think she'd like that, Dutchman?"

Dutch eyed him narrowly.

"You understand me?" Quint said. "You make me just one little piece of trouble, and you and that little lady of yours will both get some damned big trouble. You hear?"

Dutch drew breath and sighed. With his left hand, he slipped the buckle of his gun belt and let it fall.

Wade scooped it up. He grinned at Dutch. "You're not so big and mean now, are you?"

Dutch answered with a look as cutting as a fresh-honed knife.

"You know, Dutchman," Quint said, "when I sent for Easton, I figured I was getting me an ace in the hole. When he told me about meeting that little lady of yours on the coach, I seen where I had two aces. Now it looks

168

like I got me five!" He gestured at the three Tatum brothers. "Five aces beats all!"

"Five aces is a thief's hand," Dutch said.

Quint shrugged off the insult. As he turned to leave, he told the Tatums, "You boys hold him here. Keep him quiet. I got to get down and get my cattle started over onto my new range!"

CHAPTER
THIRTEEN

Once Quint was gone, Dutch spoke to the brothers. "I hope you are not sell me out cheap."

"We got a good price," Wade said harshly. He was a proud man. Dutch had injured that pride and now Wade took pleasure in revenge. But the act of treachery hadn't been easy for him. It hurt his conscience. He tried to bury the hurt under anger.

Glancing at Stony and Rob, Dutch thought they felt guilty, too. He said to them, "What price is Quint pay for your honor?"

"Dammit, it ain't like we had a choice!" Stony protested. "We need that money awful bad!"

"I pay you."

"Not enough! We got our folks and Sis to take care of! We been hard up and Pa's ailing! We couldn't hardly turn down all that money Mr. Leslie offered us! You know what I mean, don't you, Mr. Falke?"

"I know Quint Leslie stole a woman and is hold her hostage. I know he is put her into much danger. She may suffer harm, perhaps death. All of this he does to take away the land from me and destroy it for his own profit. I know that you have give me your word and now you break it. If Hannchen Gerber is hurt, the fault is with you as much as with Quint Leslie."

"It ain't right!" Rob said to his brothers. "Mr. Leslie never told us about the woman! I don't want no woman getting hurt!"

"Mr. Leslie won't let her get hurt!" Wade sounded as if he was trying to convince himself as well as his brothers.

Dutch lifted a brow at him. "Are you certain? Are you know for sure that when this is all over, he is not going to kill her? And me?"

"I don't give a damn about you!" Wade snapped at him. "I'd as soon kill you as stomp a snake!"

"Then you are going to kill me yourselves?"

"No!" Stony said before Wade could answer. "Hell, no! We don't want to kill nobody!"

"We only want to get some money and a place of our own," Rob put in. "All we want is a chance!"

Stony went on, "We can buy us a nice piece of land for the money we're getting from Mr. Leslie. Maybe we can even get us some of this good green land around here."

"You think Quint Leslie is let you take land here?" Dutch gave a shake of his head. "You think he is not take it from you and destroy it, as he now tries to take this land from me? You think he is not betray you as you now betray me?"

"*Shut up!*" Wade exploded at him.

"Dammit, I don't like none of this!" Stony said. He was carrying the shotgun he had taken from Dutch's house. He looked at it as if he had discovered he was holding a live rattler. "I don't like turning traitor and I don't like the idea of nobody getting killed and — dammit! I ain't having no more of it!"

Flinging down the gun, he headed for the brush.

"Hey!" Wade shouted. He turned to stop Stony from leaving.

As Wade's gun swung away from him, Dutch jumped. He snatched for the gun Stony had thrown down.

Rob saw the move. He lunged at Dutch.

At the same instant, Wade realized Dutch was going for the shotgun. Spinning toward Dutch, he jerked the trigger of his rifle.

The roar of the shot blasted across the river, echoing off the far bluff. It almost drowned out Rob's sudden scream. Blood blossomed on Rob's back as his leap slammed him into Dutch.

Dutch was grabbing the shotgun. As Rob struck him, he stumbled off balance. Fell. Rolling, he scrambled to his feet. He had the shotgun. His thumb hauled back the hammer and his forefinger found the trigger as he leveled it at Wade.

But Wade didn't seem to notice. He was staring at his brother. Rob lay sprawled limply on the ground.

Stony had turned back at the shot. He stood as if frozen, his eyes wide with horror as he gazed at the blood spreading on Rob's shirt.

"Rob!" Wade wailed. Dropping his rifle, he went onto his knees at Rob's side. His wail broke Stony's trance. Stony rushed to kneel by Wade. Neither paid any attention to Dutch.

172

Quint Leslie's voice came from a distance. "What's the matter? What the hell's going on up there?"

Easing down the hammer of the shotgun, Dutch made for the brush. Behind him he heard Stony gasp, "He's alive! He's still alive!"

"We got to get him back to Ma!" Wade said. "She'll know what to do!"

Dutch kept to the cover of the bushes as he worked his way to the edge of the bluff. Looking down, he saw Quint Leslie below on the bank.

Quint was on horseback. He had his revolver in his hand. He waved it as he looked up and shouted again, "What the hell's going on up there?"

From across the river, Rudd Bigelow, the Quill foreman, called, "Something wrong, boss?"

"No, dammit! Get them cattle started over!"

"They're spooky as hell!" Rudd warned. "That shot's got 'em even worse riled. They don't like shooting none at all!"

"There won't be no more shooting!" Quint snapped. He scanned the rise of the bluff. "Wade! Dammit, Wade, you there?"

He got no answer.

With a jerk of the reins, he started back along the bank, heading for the gap that would take him to the top of the bluff again.

Across the river, the cowhands began pushing the cattle toward the water.

Dutch could see Hannchen and Easton in the shadows, still well away from the herd. He figured as long as Quint didn't change his orders, the girl was safe. So he would have to keep Quint away from the men and Easton, away from any opportunity to change the orders.

He slipped back through the bushes, wanting a horse. He started for the ones Stony had left tied on the trail, but he didn't have to go that far. He found the mount Wade had been using tied close by. It was a good Falcon cow horse. Tugging loose the reins, he flung himself into the saddle.

About halfway to the gap, he turned from the trail and worked the horse into the brush. Astride, at the edge of the bluff, he knew he would be visible to the cowhands on the far bank. And well within rifle range. But the men were too busy to notice him.

They had started the cattle across. The lead steers were already in the water. So were two riders, who were keeping them headed. The other men were shoving a very reluctant string of cattle over the brink. The cattle snorted and bellowed protests as they skidded down the face of the bluff and splashed into the water. Again and again, animals tried to turn back. Shouting, cursing riders forced them on.

Quint was still on the bank. He had reached the gap and was just about to start up.

"Quint!" Dutch shouted.

With a jerk of the reins that snapped his horse into a half-rear, Quint halted. Scowling, he looked at the bluff. His gun was still in his hand. As he spotted Dutch, he whipped it up and fired.

The shot was unaimed, but Quint's hand was good. Lead sang damned close past Dutch's head. He winced at the nearness of it.

The sound of the shot rebounded between the bluffs, a wild bellowing roar.

Already upset, a lead steer decided to go back the way it had come. Other cattle tried to follow. A rider cursed as he struggled his swimming horse to the steer and fought to turn it into line again.

The confusion slowed the lead swimmers. The cattle behind them began to pile up against them. Bunching, ramming together, they tried to kick and hook at each other.

More steers attempted to break away and return to shore. Caught in the current, some were drifting swiftly downstream.

Riders from the bluff plunged their horses into the water to help hold the cattle.

Dutch had to aim carefully. He didn't want to hurt the men. Sights set, he triggered the shotgun.

The mass of shot slammed into the bunched cattle. A steer in the center of the pattern flung up its head with a frantic bellow. Blood streamed down its face. For a moment, its head was high above the others. Then it disappeared under the water.

Around it, cattle hit by the spreading pellets thrashed. Pain turned nervousness to panic. Panic spread. Suddenly the cattle were writhing, twisting, milling frantically.

On land, the cattle would have been stampeding. Caught in the water, they struggled and floundered desperately. One, then another, disappeared beneath the surface. A carcass bobbed up on the current, floating downstream.

The part of the herd still on the bank panicked. Most of the animals fought away from the bluff. Some leaped madly over, heedless of the river.

The riders still on the bluff raced to hold the herd together. The men in the river shouted for more help.

Quint Leslie stared at the chaos of cattle for one startled moment, then snapped another shot at Dutch.

"Damn you, Dutchman!" he screeched. "I'll get you for this!"

But Dutch was already wheeling his horse away from the brink. The single-barreled shotgun was empty. He had no more ammunition for it. Dropping it, he called over his shoulder, "Come ahead, Quint! Catch me! If you be able!"

The stink of blood and fear was in his nostrils as he plunged his horse away from the river. He hated what he had done. The cattle were not to blame. But there had been no other way. He had to draw Quint after him. For Hannchen's sake. And for the sake of the land.

He was certain Quint would be scrambling his mount up the bluff to give chase. Quint would be mad as hell now. Too mad to do any straight thinking. Too mad to do anything but follow.

For Dutch, the trick now would be to stay ahead. To ride for the roundup camp and keep Quint riding after him. If he could make the camp, he could get help. Armed and backed by his crew, he could turn on

Quint. Capture him. Put an end to this whole damned business. See Hannchen safe again.

If he didn't make roundup camp . . .

He didn't give any consideration to that possibility. He *had* to make it to camp.

Dutch had two advantages over Quint Leslie. The horse Dutch rode had been standing resting much of the time that Quint's mount was working. And Dutch knew the trails on this side of the river. Quint didn't.

Game trails cut through the forests, crossing the broad meadows and dipping into the ravines and climbing the rocky slopes. They twisted and turned, doubling back on each other, forking to separate, then rejoining. Dutch figured he could easily lose a pursuer among them.

But he didn't want to lose Quint. He just wanted to stay out of gun range. He had to keep Quint too excited to think out what was happening and return to the river to take advantage of the hostage held there.

In the woods, Dutch kept his mount to a traveling trot. Small things skittered away from the trail ahead of him. A jay cursed him as he passed too close to its nest.

When the forest gave way to a meadow, he paused to let the horse rest. And to let Quint move in closer. Close enough to think he was gaining on his quarry. Not close enough to use his gun.

There were whitetails grazing in the meadow as Dutch reached its edge. The deer were instantly aware of him. As he drew rein, a buck looked directly at him. Then, as if on signal, the deer were bounding away. He

177

watched their flags disappearing into the woods on the far side of the meadow.

This was their range as well as his, he thought. A man might be entitled to share it with them, but no man had the right to take it from them.

Behind him, he heard the jay shriek, cursing another intruder close to its nest. It told him where Quint was. Close enough, he decided. He plunged his horse on across the meadow.

At the far side, he looked back. He saw something moving under the trees. Slamming his horse into a gallop, he dashed into the shadows of the forest just as Quint rode onto the meadow.

Glimpsing him, Quint snapped off a shot. It was an angry, futile gesture. The slug didn't strike anywhere near Dutch.

Within cover of the forest, Dutch eased the pace, playing his mount with care. The horse had to last him. He still had a long way to go.

After a few miles, the stretch of forest ended, the land dropping abruptly into a small basin. Boulders littered its bottom and patches of scrubby brush dotted it, but there were no stands of timber to offer good cover for a horse and rider.

Dutch hesitated at its rim. Riding across it, he would be exposed to fire from the rim. But to go around, keeping to cover, would mean a long, tiring ride for horse and man. A serious delay in his reaching the roundup camp.

He had to chance going straight across.

178

He plunged the horse on down the slope into the basin. At the bottom, he urged it into a gallop.

The horse answered his hands and heels, but he could feel a slight faltering in its stride. He knew it was tiring. He couldn't keep pushing it across the basin at a gallop. It just wouldn't make it.

As he eased the horse into a trot, he felt an icy tightness along his spine, as if some instinct told him danger was too close behind him. Glancing over his shoulder, he saw Quint.

Quint had halted on the rim of the basin and was tugging his rifle from its saddle boot.

With a silent curse, Dutch scanned the land around him. There was a cluster of brush just ahead to his right. Not far beyond it was a jumble of boulders. He touched rein to his mount's neck, heading for the rocks.

Quint fired.

The ridges surrounding the basin rattled with the roar of the rifle like a rumble of thunder. Dutch felt the horse jerk under him. Its head went up, its body shifting back. Its hindquarters twitched.

Dutch realized it had been hit.

Kicking free of the stirrups, he flung himself from the saddle as the horse collapsed.

He hit ground flexing, absorbing the impact. Using the momentum of the fall, he rolled and came up onto his feet running. Lunging for the brush.

Quint's second shot slammed into the bushes ahead of Dutch. That shot had been meant as a warning, an order to Dutch to stop and surrender.

He kept going.

The rocks were too far away. He went for the thicket of brush. As he flung himself into it, sharp branches grabbed at him, snatching his sleeves and whipping across his face. With his eyes clenched shut, he forced on until he felt certain he must be well within cover. Then he dropped to his knees. Head ducked low, he opened his eyes.

He was surrounded by leafy branches. Squirming around, he cautiously pulled one aside and looked out.

He spotted Quint on the face of the downslope, the rifle in one hand, the reins in the other, as he let his mount pick its way to the bottom. Quint kept his own eyes on the brush where Dutch was hidden.

Dutch's horse was down. Its hindquarters looked lifeless, but it struggled in an attempt to get its forelegs under it and rise. He could hear the noises it made as it sucked breath. Pained, frightened noises. Terrible noises. But there was nothing he could do to help.

Easing back into the brush, he wriggled onto his belly and dug his elbows against the ground. He shoved himself along under the spreading branches, working his way to the back of the thicket. Quint had seen him go into the brush and was heading straight for him.

He had no way to fight. No weapon. His only chance was to make it unseen to some other cover. The nearest likely cover was the cluster of boulders behind the thicket. But there was a hell of a lot of open ground between him and the rocks. Too much. He couldn't run for them without Quint seeing him.

Head down, he shouted from behind the thicket, "Quint! Be decent to put the hurt horse from out its misery!"

"I'll put *you* out of your misery, Dutchman!" Quint snapped back. He sounded angry enough to mean it.

Breath held, Dutch listened intently, trying to read Quint's actions by the sounds they made. He heard Quint's horse slow. Stop. Leather creaked. That was the sound of a saddle straining as one stirrup took all of the rider's weight. Quint was dismounting.

Metallic clicking told Dutch that Quint had cocked the rifle.

To kill the downed horse, Dutch wondered, or to fire at close range into the brush?

No damned chance at all, if Quint peppered the bushes with lead —

Dutch broke for the rocks.

At the same instant, the rifle roared.

Dutch threw himself down behind the boulders. His breath was locked in his lungs, drawing a tight cramp through his chest. As he realized he had made it to fresh cover, he sighed, then sucked in another breath.

"All right, Dutchman," Quint called. "The horse is dead! Now you!"

On his belly, Dutch eased himself forward. With cautious slowness he lifted his head just enough to look over a jut of rock.

He saw Quint, afoot now, raising the butt of the rifle to his shoulder.

"Give it up, Dutchman!" Quint shouted. "You know you can't beat me! You know I don't *want* to kill you!

181

Give it up and come on out! Pack out with your hide whole while you still got the chance!"

Dutch lay silent, watching as Quint waited for some reply. From the look on Quint's face, the offer was a bluff. Quint was too angry to let him surrender and walk away.

After a moment, Quint called again, "Come on out, Dutchman!"

Again he waited for an answer. He got none.

Sighting on the thicket, he triggered the rifle.

CHAPTER
FOURTEEN

Leaves shivered as lead slammed into the bushes. Quint stood watching for some motion and listening for some sound of pain or fear from the man he thought was hidden there. The echo of the shot died and the trembling of the leaves stopped. There was only stillness, only silence.

Lying behind the boulders, Dutch considered the shots Quint had spent so far. If Quint kept shooting into the brush, he would empty the rifle. He probably had more ammunition for it. He would probably start to reload it. Dutch judged the distance between himself and Quint, wondering if he could spring across the open land and jump Quint during the time Quint was trying to reload.

It would take a hell of a quick sprint. And Quint had a revolver on his hip. He was a fast hand with it. When he saw Dutch coming, he would undoubtedly drop the rifle and go for the handgun.

The odds weren't good, Dutch decided.

Quint took a cautious step closer to the brush. Aiming the rifle, he fired again.

The echo bounded back from the walls of the basin. It was still rumbling faintly as another shot sounded. A shot from a distance.

Dust puffed from the ground a couple of strides away from Quint. Not far from the horse Quint had left ground-hitched. The horse jerked up its head and side-stepped.

Quint wheeled. The rifle was at his shoulder. He squinted over it toward the ridge he had followed Dutch down.

Frowning, Dutch squirmed to get a look at the ridge. He spotted a shadowy figure on horseback at the edge of the forest. Saw a faint trace of smoke as the rider fired again.

Another puff of dust jumped at Quint's side.

Quint snapped a shot back at the rider on the ridge, and ducked for cover. He threw himself down behind the carcass of Dutch's horse. His own mount danced nervously.

The rider on the ridge fired again.

Dutch heard the impact of the slug and knew from the sound that it had hit the body of the dead horse.

Quint's mount decided to head for safer ground. Neck twisted to keep the dragging reins from under its hoofs, it began a sidling jog. It was moving away from Quint. Heading in the direction of the boulders where Dutch lay hidden.

Quint glanced at his fleeing mount. Anxiously, he threw a shot at the rider on the ridge, then ran to catch the horse.

Dutch lunged from cover.

184

As Quint grabbed for the trailing reins, he saw Dutch coming at him. With a jerk, he brought up the gun, leveling it toward Dutch.

Dutch was in the open. Too damned close for Quint to miss him. He felt a surge of despair, of certainty that the gamble was lost. Still racing toward Quint, he tensed for the impact of the slug.

With the rifle at his hip, Quint closed his finger on the trigger.

Nothing happened.

Quint's forehead creased with puzzlement. Then understanding spread across his face. He had failed to cock the gun. He pumped the lever.

As the lever clicked, Dutch was leaping.

The rifle blasted.

But Dutch was past the muzzle of the gun, his body ramming against Quint's. He could feel the heat of the explosion as his side brushed the barrel.

He had escaped the shot. He was still alive — and fighting!

Quint reeled back as Dutch struck him. Quick-footed, he caught his balance. Dutch's right hand was grabbing the gun. His left clenched, driving for Quint's belly. Quint twisted away as the fist landed. The blow glanced off his ribs.

Sudden pain startled Dutch. It speared from the joint of his right shoulder, streaking down his arm. He had forgotten the accident with Hannchen's luggage. He had assumed the injury was minor, healed now. The pain told him he had been mistaken. There was still some unhealed damage. A devil hiding in his shoulder.

Teeth clenched, he tried to ignore the pain. He had a grip on the barrel of the rifle. Quint was pulling back, trying to tug the gun away from him. He couldn't let Quint get it. He slapped his left hand over the action and wrenched against Quint's pull.

Quint turned the pull to a sudden shove. For an instant, Dutch was falling backward. As he danced to get his feet under him again, Quint kicked at him. A hard sharp-toed boot slammed into his shin. It almost drove his leg from under him.

As he felt the shock of pain in the bone and the flexing of his knee, Dutch threw himself forward, into Quint.

Quint staggered as Dutch's weight hit him, but he managed to catch his footing. Braced, both men clung to the rifle in an almost motionless struggle.

The gun wasn't cocked. For all Dutch knew, it might even be empty. Still, it could be a formidable weapon. The muzzle, rammed sharply into a man's gut, could drive the breath or even the life out of him. The butt, swung as a club, could crack his skull.

Neither man dared ease his grip for fear that the other might get control of the weapon.

Dutch was much younger than Quint. He was taller and heavier and stronger. But the devil in his shoulder fought against him.

And the proud anger burning in Quint gave him an animal ferocity beyond his normal strength.

Momentarily, they were matched. Deadlocked.

Dutch could feel the tension of the muscles that pulled from his right hand to his elbow to his shoulder,

186

tearing at the injured joint. The pain was increasing, the arm weakening. He felt his fingers about to tremble, and knew he wouldn't be able to maintain his grip much longer.

He knew that Quint, too, was weakening. Quint's face was red with effort and his breath was coming in hard gasps. His eyes flashed with desperation.

Dutch sensed that he was about to make a move.

Suddenly Quint shifted weight and swung up a knee. He drove it between Dutch's legs.

Anticipating, Dutch flinched away an instant before the knee hit. It struck his thigh, ramming hard, jolting his leg.

With a shriek, as if the knee had found its target, Dutch let go the rifle and gripped himself. Bent low, he moaned like a man in severe pain.

Quint had the gun. He grinned as he cocked it. Totally confident, he took his time, savoring his victory.

Dutch jumped. He threw himself in under the gun barrel. His head rammed into Quint's belly. He felt the shock of the impact run down his spine, and heard the breath gust out of Quint.

Even as he doubled over, falling backward, Quint tried to strike out. He lashed at Dutch's head with the gun barrel.

The blow was weak. Dutch was already twisting away. The gun barely glanced against his cheek. He hardly noticed it.

Quint slammed to the ground, flat on his back.

Dutch was taking no chances. He flung himself down on Quint's chest. His hands went for Quint's throat.

187

There wasn't much breath in Quint. The thumbs that pressed against his Adam's apple stopped him from getting more. His face darkened. His mouth worked as he tried to drag air into his lungs. Then his eyes glazed and his struggles weakened.

At last he lay still.

Through the fingers on Quint's throat, Dutch could tell that this was no bluff. He eased back. His shoulder ached like hell. A sudden weariness that was close to exhaustion swept through him. Slowly, he rose to his knees astraddle Quint.

Quint's body spasmed as the lungs gasped for air, but that was the only motion.

Dutch picked up the rifle. He set the butt against the ground and braced against the gun as he got himself to his feet. His own lungs worked violently for breath. He could feel his heart hammering against his ribs. His whole being begged for rest.

But it wasn't done yet. There were still Quill cattle moving onto Falcon range. And there was a rider galloping toward Dutch. As he heard the hoofbeats behind him, he remembered the rider on the ridge. The one who had helped him when Quint had him at gunpoint.

A friend, he thought. But instinctively his hands were cocking the rifle and lifting the muzzle as he turned toward the oncoming rider.

With a start, he recognized the figure on the running horse. It was Rosy Tatum.

She was sitting astride a man's saddle on a mount that Dutch didn't recognize. Her face glistened with tears. Her voice caught in her throat as she called, "Are you all right, Mr. Falke? Please God! Are you all right?"

"*Ja.*" He nodded, astonished by her presence.

She hauled back on the reins. The horse was heavily lathered, with foam flagging from its mouth. Excited by the shooting and the wild run across the basin, it was unwilling to stop. It fought the bit. Dutch snatched the bridle, helping Rosy bring it to a halt.

Her skirts were an awkward burden as she started to dismount. When she threw a leg over the cantle, the nervous horse shied. Off balance, she tottered far to the side, looking about to fall.

Dutch flung down the rifle and grabbed for her. Fresh pain flashed through his aching shoulder as he caught her in his arms. Ignoring it, he held her while she freed her foot from the high stirrup. Then he set her down. As her feet touched the ground, she leaned against him. Sobbing, she pressed her face into his chest.

He closed his arms around her, holding her, feeling the warmth of her body against his. For that moment, nothing mattered but the girl in his arms. He wanted to comfort her. Softly, he said, "Do not worry. All is right now."

She caught a breath and looked up into his face. "Are you sure?"

"Yes," he replied. But it wasn't all right. He had turned his back on Quint Leslie. Releasing Rosy, he wheeled to look at Quint.

The rancher was still lying limp on the ground. There was color in his face now. A little too much color, Dutch thought. He glimpsed a faint flutter of Quint's eyelashes. And he was certain Quint's hand hadn't been outstretched that way before. Not reaching toward the rifle Dutch had dropped.

Scooping up the gun, Dutch raised it as if to club the butt down on Quint's head.

Reflexively, Quint rolled back and threw an arm up to protect his face.

Dutch shifted the gun, his finger finding the trigger. He pointed the muzzle at Quint's chest.

Quint met his eyes and growled hoarsely, "You ain't won yet, Dutchman. You got me, but I still got that little Dutch bride of yours, and my men are still pushing Quill cattle onto your range. Are you as good as your word, Dutchman? Or are you a damned liar? You promised if I got a herd bedded on your range, you'd give up to me."

"Yes," Dutch admitted. He might have Quint, but Quint still had a handful of aces. "Stand up!"

Quint dragged himself to his feet.

"Take from off the neck the bandanna," Dutch told him. As he obeyed, Dutch said to Rosy, "Take the bandanna and tie his hands behind him. Tie tight the knots."

Rosy moved cautiously. Dutch held the rifle ready while she took the bandanna. Watching Dutch's eyes, Quint crossed his wrists behind him.

As Rosy was tying them, Dutch asked her, "How are you here when I need you?"

"It was on account of the way Stony was acting in town. It just didn't seem right. I got to worrying and I

190

— uh — well, I tooken a horse and lit out to catch up to you. Only by the time I got there, Rob had got shot —" She caught a sobbing breath. "Wade shot him! That damn fool Wade!"

"He was intend to shoot me," Dutch said.

She nodded. "The *damn fool!*"

"All a bunch of damn fools," Quint grumbled.

Dutch asked her, "Is hurt bad, the brother Rob?"

"No. Wade and Stony got a travvy rigged up to take him to Ma. She'll get him patched up all right." She finished tying Quint's wrists and stepped aside.

Dutch examined the knots. They were good.

Rosy went on, "I could see Rob wasn't too bad off, and Stony told me how Mr. Leslie was chasing after you, and you without no gun or nothing. I thought — I was afraid of what might happen to you. I figured — like you said — we owed you!"

"You should've stayed out of this," Quint told her. "It ain't none of your business. You'll pay for butting in."

She answered him with a dark glare, and said to Dutch, "Is there anything else I can do to help?"

He glanced off in the direction of the roundup camp. It lay at a distance beyond the far rim of the basin.

The horses had both run off. Rosy's mount had found graze close by and stopped to eat. Quint's horse had gone farther before it stopped. He figured he would need both horses. Gesturing at the rim of the basin, he asked her, "Can you walk that far?"

"Sure!"

"Go, build on the rim a fire. A very smoky fire. Someone from the Falcon crew will come to see what is burning. Tell him you must speak to Slim Walker. Tell Slim what is happen. Tell him to bring men with guns to the river, quick. Understand?"

"Uh huh."

"But first, you please keep watch on him" — he nodded at Quint — "while I catch the horses. Yes?"

"Be glad to!" She picked up the rifle she had used to fire at Quint from the edge of the forest. After checking and cocking it, she leveled it at Quint's gut.

He looked at it and then at her face, judging her. The slump of his shoulders said he had seen the ability in her to use the rifle if she felt it was necessary.

Dutch caught the horse Rosy had ridden easily enough. On it, he rounded up Quint's mount. After he checked the gun he found a box full of ammunition in Quint's saddle-bags. He replaced the spent rounds. Then he had Quint climb onto Rosy's horse, and took Quint's mount for himself. A familiar horse could be an advantage to a prisoner. He didn't want Quint having any advantages. The game was still far from won.

CHAPTER
FIFTEEN

Dutch didn't trust his prisoner. He carried the rifle across his saddlebow with its muzzle pointed at Quint.

Quint kept eying it askance, as if he was wondering how he might turn it on Dutch.

"Who is Easton?" Dutch asked him.

"A hard, tough man."

"A hired killer?"

"No, not that. He don't like killing. He don't do it unless there ain't no other way. His business is finding ways around killing. He'd sooner use his brain than a gun."

"He is one who makes a plan?"

"Yeah."

"It is his plan to steal Hannchen?"

"Steal what?"

"Hannchen Gerber. The woman."

"That little Dutchie? Yeah. That was a real piece of luck," Quint said, "him running into her on the coach like that, and her telling him all about the wedding with you. That's when he come up with this whole idea, then and there."

"It is Easton's idea to move your cattle onto my range?" Dutch asked.

"Hell, no! That was my idea! I only just hired him to find a good way of doing it without a lot of killing. That bet I made with you was his idea. Me, now, I'd 've liked to come in shooting, and take what I want. Ten, fifteen years ago, that's how I'd 've done it. That's what I should've done when I first come here." Quint sighed. Wistfully, he added, "I took me a good piece of range in Texas that way a time back."

"Why are you not stay there?"

"The land played out. I had to move on."

And he would have to keep moving on, Dutch thought, if he kept destroying the land by overgrazing and stripping it. Moving on and on and on until there was no place left to go.

Quint was still talking. "Trouble nowadays is there's too damn much law around!"

"Sam Steele?" Dutch asked with surprise. Steele belonged to Quint. Even if he didn't, he wouldn't present a man like Quint Leslie with much of a problem.

"Steele? Hell, he ain't nothing but a joke!" Quint replied. "It's the damned federal marshals you got to worry about now. A man does a little killing nowadays, and the next thing he knows, he's got a lot of explaining to do, maybe even got troopers all over his place. Too damned much trouble. Easton promised me he could get me your range without doing nothing that would bring the law into it."

"By stealing a woman?"

"Far as she knows, she ain't been stole. She ran away with him of her own will. She's staying with him for today while he sees to it a job gets done. She thinks once the job's done, he's gonna take her off and marry her."

"But you hold her hostage. You are threaten to harm her if I do not let you put the cattle onto my range. If she is hurt, then the law comes."

Quint shook his head. "If there was to be a lot of shooting and that little Dutchie happened to get a bullet in her, it'd be hard for anybody to say which side the bullet come from. Since she'd be with my crew, it'd sure look like it was a Falcon bullet that got her. It'd be *you* who'd be explaining to the law, not *me*."

"Still, there would be the federal marshal. There would be much to explain for everyone."

"I don't think that's gonna happen. I don't reckon you'd like it much if your little bride got buried before the wedding, eh, Dutchman?"

Dutch didn't reply. He had to admit to himself that Quint was right. Hannchen was his responsibility. He couldn't let her be harmed. Even if it cost him the land, he had to protect her.

They could hear the splashing and bawling of the cattle in the river, and the shouting and cursing of the cowhands driving them, before they reached the bluff-top trail. At the point where the Tatums had been, Dutch stopped.

The brothers were gone, but they had left their mark. They had trampled a broad area of brush all the way to the rim of the bluff. Halting at the edge of the open area, Dutch ordered Quint to dismount.

Quint stepped stiffly from his horse, stretched, then walked to the brink and looked down into the river. Dutch swung from the saddle and followed him, keeping the rifle pointed at him.

"They ain't done a hell of a lot since I left," Quint grumbled. "Ought to 've got them all across and half bedded by now."

"They had trouble," Dutch said as he stepped to Quint's side.

The Quint hands had obviously had a lot of trouble getting the mill broken and the cattle under control. Less than half the herd was bunched on the bank under the bluff. Riders in the water were fighting more across, and on the far bank still more were yet to be shoved into the river. The riders and their mounts looked near exhaustion.

Harrumphing, Quint said, "Hell, you can't get a damn day's work for a wage if you don't ride herd on the men yourself."

That was a poor thing for a rancher to admit, Dutch thought. If a man had the respect of a good crew, they treated him fairly. And in any case, the Quill riders shouldn't be faulted for the work they had done. They'd had their hands full when the cattle paincked in the water. They had brought the herd under control and were getting them across. What more could Quint ask of them?

Dutch spotted Rudd Bigelow among the men in the water. He said to Quint, "Call your foreman. Tell him you be want the girl brought out."

196

Quint looked over his shoulder at Dutch. "Why the hell should I?"

"When I am have her safe here, I will make you free. If she is be hurt, I will make you hurt. Understand?"

Scowling, Quint worked his jaw as he considered Dutch's threat.

Suddenly brush rustled behind Dutch. At the sound, he wheeled. He found himself looking into the barrel of a revolver. It was leveled at his chest. The man holding it was James Easton.

"Drop the gun, Dutchman," Easton said, stepping from the bushes where he had been hidden.

In one long look, Dutch gauged Easton. The man was tense, his neck corded and his mouth set. There was sweat beaded on his forehead. His finger on the trigger was already exerting a light pressure. Just a little more pull would release the hammer.

Easton might prefer not to kill, but his eyes said he was ready to do it.

Dutch let the rifle slide out of his hands.

Quint began to laugh. There was a wild edge to his cackling, a frantic relief at the release of the fear that had been in him.

"Leslie, you're a fool!" Easton snapped.

Quint stopped laughing. He glared at Easton.

Easton went on, "You hired me to do a job. You should have left it all in my hands. But no! You had to keep giving orders, trying to run it your way. You had to go chasing all over and get yourself into the fire. You're lucky I've pulled you out now."

"I can take care of myself!" Quint growled at him.

"Can you?" Scorn dripped from Easton's voice.

Quint wasn't willing to admit a mistake. "You just untie me! I'll show you!"

The gun, the power, was in Easton's hands. Dutch interrupted, asking him, "Where is Hannchen?"

"She's safe enough."

"You will return her to me?"

Easton didn't reply. He flicked his eyes toward Quint and ordered, "Untie him."

Quint was facing Easton. Dutch started to step behind him. Easton snapped, "No! Not like that! Turn around, Leslie. Don't let him get you between us!"

Quint turned, offering his bound hands to Dutch. Dutch fumbled with the knots in the bandanna holding his wrists. Quint had been trying to work his hands free. He had only succeeded in pulling the knots impossibly tight.

Dutch said, "I will have to cut this."

Warily, Easton asked him, "You have a knife?"

He nodded.

"Use it, then."

Dutch moved slowly as he pulled his barlow knife from a pocket. He bit it open, then slipped the blade between the bandanna and Quint's arm. As he sawed at the cloth, Quint said, "Easy there, don't cut me."

"Hurry it up!" Easton said. His voice ground through his throat. Dutch darted a quick glance at him. It was obvious he didn't like the gun he held. He would have preferred some subtle mental trickery to a physical confrontation. He stood braced, every muscle taut. A

198

pulse throbbed in his temple. The hand holding the revolver quivered slightly.

Dutch could feel a trembling in his own gut. He drew breath slowly, holding himself steady. If his estimate of Easton was wrong, or Easton's luck was good, he might very soon be dead.

It was the chance he had to take.

He jabbed the point of the knife into Quint's arm. At the same time, he grabbed Quint's elbow with his other hand. Quint squealed as the knife drew blood: Dutch wrenched at him, twisting him around to thrust him toward Easton. It was all one move. Dutch jumped as he threw Quint off balance and shoved him at Easton.

Easton had been ready for Dutch to try something. Too ready. His finger was very tight on the trigger, and his nerves were just as tight. At Dutch's sudden move, he jerked the trigger. His hand flinched as the gun bucked in it.

The shot went wild.

Quint fell to the ground.

As Easton thumbed back the hammer to try again, Dutch lunged.

He went in low, diving for Easton's legs. Startled, Easton jumped back. Impulsively, he swung the revolver, trying to club Dutch with it.

The swing was wide. The muzzle of the gun grazed Dutch's shoulder. The shock of pain Dutch felt was out of proportion to the strength of the blow. It radiated from the sore shoulder through his whole body. He winced, his knees buckling.

Easton had managed to cock the gun. As Dutch fell, he was firing.

Dutch felt the nearness of the slug. Felt the impact as it hit the earth barely inches from him. He was rolling. Twisting. Grabbing for Easton's ankle.

Both hands caught Easton's leg. Still rolling, Dutch tugged hard. Easton tried again to smash the gun at his head, but his leg was being jerked from under him.

As Easton fell, Dutch scrambled to his knees. He threw himself across Easton, both hands locking on the revolver. With a wrench, he broke Easton's grip on it. And slammed it down on Easton's head.

Easton went limp.

Shifting his grip on the gun, Dutch started to rise. He had his forefinger on the trigger. His thumb was drawing back the hammer as he came up onto his feet.

"Drop it, Dutchman!" Quint Leslie snarled behind his back.

The tone told him it was no bluff. Quint was behind him with a weapon aimed at him.

He could feel the tension of the hammer under his thumb. He knew he could spin and let the pin drop and send a shot at Quint. But in the instant it would take him to do it, Quint could put a slug into him. And that wouldn't help Hannchen at all.

He eased the hammer down and let the revolver slide from his fingers. Raising his hands shoulder high, he turned slowly to face Quint.

Quint had managed to work free of the bonds that had held him. He was holding the rifle. The same one

200

Dutch had held on him during the long ride. Now it was pointed at Dutch's gut.

"I got the winning hand now, Dutchman!" Quint said with a sharp laugh.

He gave a nod toward the river, where Quill cattle were bellowing and riders were shouting. It sounded as if the noise of Easton's shots had gotten the herd upset and the riders had their hands full preventing another mill. It might mean a delay for Quill, but only a small one. Judging from the sounds, Quill cattle would be pushing onto Falcon range very soon.

Dutch eyed the rifle, wondering if Rosy had given his message to Slim Walker. Maybe his own men were on the way now, ready to fight. But what could they do while both he and Hannchen were Quint Leslie's prisoners?

Damned little, he was afraid.

Quint said, "Hear them beefs? Sounds like they're most all on this side of the river now, don't it? Like they're moving right along on the way to Falcon range. You want to come see the last hand played, Dutchman? Come watch while I win."

His grin was wide and smug. He kept the rifle steady. There was no trembling in his hands. He gave a nod for Dutch to follow as he back-stepped toward the rim of the bluff.

Suddenly, he was tottering. The rifle was waving wildly. Unintentionally, as he tried for balance, he triggered it.

At the blast, Dutch ducked. He scooped up the revolver and swung its muzzle toward Quint.

But Quint was gone.

From the riverbank below, a man shouted in horror. Others echoed the shout. The bellowing of the cattle became frantic.

Holding the gun loosely in his hand, Dutch stepped to the edge of the bluff. A big chunk of the rim was gone, crumbled away. Cautiously, he leaned forward to look down.

The Quill riders had gotten all of the herd across. Most of the cattle were bunched up on the bank directly below, a tight, milling mass of sharp-spined backs and long-pointed horns.

The riders threading among them were no longer trying to hold and control the cattle. Now the men were forcing into the herd, breaking it up and driving bunches back, away from the bluff. They were letting the spooked animals run. Some plunged into the river, trying to swim to the far shore again. No cowhand attempted to stop them. The men were working toward another goal.

Drawing a deep breath, Dutch watched the men open a space in the mass of cattle at the foot of the bluff. As the space widened, he saw a figure on the ground. It looked like the tattered remains of an abandoned scarecrow. A hoof-battered, horn-pierced, broken thing.

With awe, Dutch thought of the many years Quint Leslie had abused the land, ravaging it, destroying it. Now the land had taken revenge. It had thrown him under the hoofs of the herd he had meant to use against it. It had killed him with his own greed.

202

As the first of the cowhands reached the body and dismounted, Dutch wheeled away from the sight below.

In the instant that he turned, he glimpsed a muzzle flash, heard a shot, felt the sudden snap as lead seared across his chest.

He saw Easton on his belly on the ground, braced on his elbows with a tiny over-under hide-out gun held steady in both hands. He saw the hatred in Easton's face, and the gloating certainty that the shot would find its mark. He sensed that if he had turned a moment later, the slug would have hit squarely in his back instead of skimming his chest.

His own action was instinctive. There was a gun in his own hand. It whipped up, throwing lead in reply.

Easton was already squeezing the trigger on the second barrel of the hide-out gun as Dutch's slug hit him. He jerked at the impact, looking as if he was trying to leap from the ground. Then he sprawled, his hands still clutching the hide-out gun. His fingers loosened, and the little gun fell from them. His face pressed to the earth that was slowly soaking up his blood. He lay still, looking empty and shrunken within his clothing.

Dutch sensed a second shot wasn't necessary. James Easton would never be a danger to anyone again.

CHAPTER
SIXTEEN

Easton's shot had skimmed close enough to leave a tear in Dutch's vest and a stinging trail across his chest, but it hadn't broken the skin. There was no blood.

As he examined the damage, Dutch caught the sounds of galloping horses in the distance. That would be Slim with the Falcon crew, he thought.

He called out to the Quill riders on the bank below. The foreman, Rudd Bigelow, answered him. He said to Bigelow, "Quint Leslie is dead."

Bigelow nodded. Even at the distance, Dutch could see the shocked pallor of his face. His boss had died in a rough way.

Dutch told him, "James Easton also is dead."

"What?"

"Easton is dead. Here on the bluff. And my men come now. We can fight against you. Will you go to fight for dead men?"

Bigelow looked around at the other Quill hands. They were all working cowboys, not hired guns. They had done a hard day's work. They were water-soaked, weary men astride fagging horses. But they obeyed orders. None spoke in reply to the question in

Bigelow's eyes. It was up to the foreman to make the decision.

Quint Leslie had bought loyalty from his men. He had never earned it. Bigelow said, "I reckon there ain't much good in fighting and dying for a dead man."

"Yes," Dutch agreed. He could sympathize with the men on the bank below. He told them, "Tend the dead. Bed the cattle on the grass and make here your camp. My men come and help. Yes?"

"You're the boss now." Bigelow touched his hat brim to Dutch. He knew the bet. Dutch had won Quill's range and cattle and crew.

"Where is the woman?" Dutch asked.

"She's over on the other side, waiting for Easton. You want us to fetch her to you?"

Dutch sighed. No matter what his own feelings might be, he had a debt to Herr Onkel Heinrich, and an obligation to Hannchen Gerber. "I go to her."

But first he had to see Slim and explain what had happened. He swung up onto Quint's horse and rode out to meet the approaching riders.

Slim Walker was in the lead, with Rosy Tatum riding at his side. Rosy was astraddle the sorrel filly. At the sight of Dutch, she gigged it into a hard run.

"Are you all right, Mr. Falke?" she called.

He nodded. They drew rein side by side, and he told her, "I am very tired. The fight is done."

Slim halted before him. "Done? What you mean, boss?"

Dutch explained tersely, telling Slim to give the Quill crew a hand with the cattle. Then he asked Rosy, "Where are you find that horse?"

"One of the fellers caught her running loose. I hope you don't mind me riding her. I know she's something special to you."

"It is well," he said, thinking that Rosy was something special, too.

He led his crew to the gap down the face of the bluff. As his crew joined the Quill riders, he dismounted and loosened his cinches. Rosy sat the filly and watched in silence as he remounted and plunged his horse into the river.

He was almost across when he realized someone was behind him. Rosy Tatum. She had her skirts pulled up above her knees, and was driving the filly through the water with determination.

"Where you go?" he called to her.

"With you!"

"I go to my bride."

She didn't answer, but kept on after him.

The cattle pounding down the bluff had beaten its face into a climbable slope. Dutch scrambled his horse up. At the top, he waited.

Rosy handled the filly well. She pushed it up the bluff and halted at Dutch's side.

He looked at her, at the brightness of her eyes and the excited flush of her cheeks, and the full ripe warmth of her mouth. Slowly, he said, "You must be go back."

She shook her head.

206

"You can come no more with me. I must go on to Hannchen."

Her eyes stayed on his a moment more. They glistened damply. Swallowing, she lowered them.

Dutch turned away from her. Nudging his mount's flanks, he rode toward the woods. This time, she did not follow.

He found Hannchen afoot, her horse tied in the brush. She was sitting waiting on a windfall. When she saw him she gathered her skirts and started toward him.

The afternoon was old and the shadows were dusky. It was obvious that she did not recognize him at first. She thought him a Quill rider there in the half-dark under the trees. As she realized her mistake, she drew back and he could sense the fear in her.

He would speak with her in German now, he thought. Gently, he called, "Do not be afraid. I will not hurt you."

She looked frantically around, as if hunting a way of escaping him, or someone to defend her against him. Finding no help and no escape, she stood with her shoulders slumping like a child awaiting punishment.

"I will not hurt you," he repeated. He halted before her and stepped down from the saddle to face her.

She looked through her lowered lashes at him. Faintly, she said, "I did not mean to do wrong, Herr Falke. But — but —"

"You are waiting here for Easton?"

She hesitated. Slowly, she admitted, "Yes." And then she blurted, "He *loves* me! Love! It is a wonderful

207

thing! I — he — we — I know it is wrong! I was sent to you. But I met him! I cannot — it is — can you understand?"

"Yes," he said softly.

"Will you . . . ?" Her voice trailed off, her question not completed. A frown wrinkled her brow. "What is it? What is so wrong?"

"Easton is dead."

"Oh no!" She flung herself against Dutch, her face pressing into his chest. His injured shoulder ached as he held her, letting her cry in his arms.

For a few minutes, her sobs were wild, uncontrolled. Then she managed to catch breath. Thinly, she said, "I want to go home!"

"I will take you home now." He pulled from her arms and started for the tied horse.

She snatched his sleeve. "*Home!* Home to my mother and father!"

He looked down into her tear-streaked face. "You mean to Hesse? You mean that you do not want to stay here and marry me?"

"I — I — please! I'm sorry, Herr Falke, but it is not what I thought, this America of yours! It is not so — I want to go home!"

"Yes," he said with gentle sympathy for the child who had expected to find a land of fairy tales come true. "Come. We will return to the ranch now. You can rest. Tomorrow, I'll make the arrangements. You will go home."

★   ★   ★

208

It was completely dark when they reached the ranch house. Dutch was surprised to see lamplight glowing through the windows. It occurred to him that the English woman must have gotten back to the ranch. She was probably waiting inside to express her opinions. He braced himself for the encounter.

But as he and Hannchen drew rein in front of the house, it was Rosy Tatum who came out to greet them.

Swinging down from the saddle, Dutch said to her, "I was think you have gone back to your family."

"I figured you might need me here," she told him. Then she turned to Hannchen. "Your English lady friend is inside. She's been having fits worrying over you. She's tooken to bed like she was purely sick."

"Ach, Frau Prescott!" Hannchen gasped. Dutch helped her from her horse. As she scurried into the house, she was saying, "She is worry so much over all things! Poor Frau Prescott!"

Dutch and Rosy stood facing each other. He said, "Hannchen is to go home to Hesse. She wants her family."

"Then you're not gonna marry her?"

"No." It was too dark for him to read Rosy's expression, but he thought he heard an edge of pleasure in her voice. He asked, "Are you not go back to your family?"

"Don't you want me to stay here?"

"Yes."

"Then I reckon they'll have to get along without me."

209

Hoping he understood her correctly, and that she would understand him, he said, "The filly you rode, she is to be a present for my bride. Will you take her?"

Rosy understood. He could hear it in her voice as she replied, "I'd be right proud to!"